Jill stood still

Had she moved the rocker to the room's front window last weekend? Her heart skipped a beat as she stared at it.

Almost imperceptibly, it appeared to be moving…as in those moments after someone has gotten up and walked away.

You really need more sleep. Next you'll be seeing apparitions in the hallway and bogeymen in your closet.

It was only the wind, of course. Drafts found their way into the old house whenever the wind blew outside.

A faint sound echoed down the shotgun hallway leading to the front entry. Jill looked down, surprised to see her hands clenched.

It's only my imagination.

Or Sheriff Johnson, here to give her a logical explanation for the lights at Warren's house.

She strode to the front door, already forming an apology, and pulled it open.

"I suppose it was n-nothing…"

She stammered to a halt, her hand at her throat, and stared into the face of the man who'd sworn he'd never set foot on Chapel Hill again.

Dear Reader,

Beautiful northern Wisconsin...just the words make me think of pine-scented breezes, sparkling sapphire lakes and blazing fall colors. But even the loveliest places have their darker side, and that's definitely true for the little town of Blackberry Hill.

Blackberry Hill Memorial is a small, struggling hospital facing serious challenges, and the residents of this town face them, as well. For Dr. Jill Edwards and her husband, Grant, their troubled marriage may provide a perfect opportunity for an old enemy to seek revenge...and for an old ghost to find peace at last. For Grace Fisher, retirement is just ahead—only now she finds herself with a troubled teenage nephew to raise and a chance for her own once-in-a-lifetime love. Who knew life could change so quickly?

I love writing stories that touch on the lives of families of every generation and the problems so many of us face. But above all, I love writing about men and women who must overcome nearly insurmountable obstacles in search of love and commitment.

I hope you enjoy Jill and Grant's story, and that you'll come back to the third in the BLACKBERRY HILL MEMORIAL series in August. If you missed the first book in the series, *Almost a Family,* you can find it at www.eHarlequin.com.

I love hearing from readers at www.roxannerustand.com, www.booksbyrustand.com or at P.O. Box 2550, Cedar Rapids, Iowa 52406-2550. Send a SASE and I'll send you bookmarks or other promotional material.

Wishing you all the best for your own happily ever after!

Roxanne Rustand

A MAN SHE CAN TRUST

Roxanne Rustand

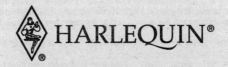

HARLEQUIN®

TORONTO • NEW YORK • LONDON
AMSTERDAM • PARIS • SYDNEY • HAMBURG
STOCKHOLM • ATHENS • TOKYO • MILAN • MADRID
PRAGUE • WARSAW • BUDAPEST • AUCKLAND

ISBN 0-373-71327-4

A MAN SHE CAN TRUST

Copyright © February 2006 by Roxanne Rustand.

Books by Roxanne Rustand

HARLEQUIN SUPERROMANCE

With love to Larry, Andy, Brian and Emily.
I am so proud of all of you!

ACKNOWLEDGMENTS

With many thanks to Rene Miller for her research assistance
into small-town law practices, Michelle Klosterman, R.N.
CEN (Certified in Emergency Nursing), whose expertise in
the operation of small-town hospitals has been invaluable,
and to Lyn Cote for your friendship and your assistance with
details of life in northern Wisconsin!

PROLOGUE

HE WAS LATE again…and this time, she knew why.

Jill dropped her gaze from the mantel clock to the dying embers in the fireplace, her fingers pressed deep into the back of her husband's leather recliner.

Her stomach pitched at the sound of a car door slamming outside. She nearly turned away and headed for the open staircase, knowing there'd still be a measure of security and comfort in feigning ignorance.

Dreading the confrontation to come.

Knowing that it was long overdue.

And well-aware that she deserved better than evenings alone and whispered conjecture among the people she passed on the streets of Blackberry Hill.

Some of her patients at the clinic knew. She'd seen the nervous darting of their eyes and their tentative, sympathetic smiles.

She'd even caught some of the rumors in the aisles of Crupper's Family Grocery on Main, when the gossips hadn't realized she was one aisle over. *Sad, isn't it? A handsome couple like that. Goes to show money and fancy degrees don't guarantee happiness.*

But it wasn't just the rumors and sympathy. It was everything else over the past two years that had undermined what they'd once had, until now they were strangers living under the same roof.

Grant's keys jingled outside the front entryway. The door swung open and he walked inside, dropped his briefcase on the antique settee and started down the wide central hallway leading past the parlor and dining room to the kitchen and den.

"Grant."

He faltered and turned, one brow raised in surprise. "You're up late," he said.

"Or early. It's already two-thirty, Grant. Where have you been?"

"It was my day to be at the Kendrick office." Irritation flickered in his dark, handsome face. "You know how far that is."

"Two hours." She took a deep breath. "And you're usually back by seven-thirty. I was worried about you, so I called your brother. He said you were both done at the courthouse by five, but you didn't go back to his office."

"As if he knew." Grant lowered his voice. "He sure as hell wasn't there. He took off for the golf course."

Before, she'd just felt anxiety over this inevitable meeting. Now, anger gnawed at her and her heart beat at a dizzying pace. "He *was* there, at seven. You weren't. He forgot his billfold."

Grant spun on his heel and strode into the parlor to within a few feet of her, a muscle ticking at the side of his jaw. "So, Detective Jill on the case. Assuming the worst."

"It's a little hard to ignore the rumors flying around this town. It's even harder to ignore the way people glance at me and look away, as if they're wondering when the poor, stupid wife is going to catch on."

His dark brown eyes glittered. "To what, Jill? Say it."

"You've been late five nights out of seven the past week. When you're here, you may as well not be— you're a million miles away. You've been seen with that red-haired woman in your car on back country roads. And," Jill added bitterly, "this entire town seemed to know what was going on *weeks* before I ever caught on."

His voice dropped another level—a sure sign of his anger. "So you've accused, tried and convicted me. Without saying a word. Without asking me a thing."

"It doesn't take much imagination. I sit in this house alone, night after night after night."

"Then you ought to be happy. You sure put yourself and this heap of rubble above anything I want."

"That's hardly fair."

"Isn't it?" He cursed under his breath. "It's all

about you, Jill. Always. We moved three times to accommodate med school, your internship and your residency. I was glad to do it, if it made you happy. Then we moved here so I could help my dad, and I wanted a nice place in town. One that wouldn't consume every last second of my time just trying to make it livable. I want a family. Except it's *still* just all about you."

Afraid to say a word, she felt as if she was teetering at the edge of a precipice with jagged glass waiting far below.

"You got what you wanted," he continued, the absence of emotion and the cold, flat expression in his eyes more chilling than outright anger. "In every way. You got your career. You got this damned house—a place that's done nothing but drive us further apart. And that little inconvenience of an unexpected pregnancy? *Gone.*"

She winced. "That's so unfair. So totally cruel and unfair."

"Unfair?" He bit out the word. "Would you have lost that baby if you'd listened to me? You always do what *you* want, no matter what anyone says. And as for this marriage? I think we know what's left of it. If you've got to ask if I've cheated on you, then we are truly over."

She glared at him, stunned by his attack. "I shouldn't have to ask."

"For what it's worth, I haven't." Their eyes locked in anger. Then he took a step away. "I'll be back tomorrow for my things."

He grabbed his briefcase and headed for the entryway. The door crashed against the wall as he went out.

And just that fast, he was gone—but it wasn't a surprise.

Earlier tonight, after talking to Phil, she'd been worried. Grant was lean, hard-muscled. He'd started running four miles a day and lifting weights after his father had his first heart attack at fifty, and was in superb condition. But as a physician, she knew even young, healthy males could keel over. And seeing sick people day after day made her all the more aware of the risks.

So she'd driven to town, expecting Grant had come back from Kendrick to put in some hours at his father's law office. Wanting to check on him…though maybe that had just been an excuse.

On the way, she'd imagined that he might tear himself away from his work, so they could go to a quiet little restaurant for a late supper and a chance to visit, away from the battlefield of home.

A chance, perhaps, to heal their latest rift over her plans to remodel their old Victorian.

His car had been behind the office just as she'd thought. She'd gone to the back and tried the doorknob. And then she'd heard the voices. Grant's laughter. The sultry voice of a woman.

The lights inside had dimmed.

And with them, her last hopes for her marriage died.

CHAPTER ONE

"YOU TWO MADE one hell of a mistake, Missy." Warren waggled a gnarled forefinger under Dr. Jill Edwards's nose, his faded blue eyes fixed on hers with steely resolve. "It isn't too late."

Jill smiled patiently as she finished checking the surgical site on his chest, listened to his heart sounds then draped the stethoscope around her neck. She pulled the covers up to his shoulders. "That's the most optimistic thinking I've heard from you yet, Warren. Given that your son and I have been separated for four months and that he lives two hours away."

"But you're not *divorced*," he countered triumphantly. "Now, why is that?"

"I'm sure we'll get to it…soon. Very soon."

"He's a *lawyer*. Could have done it right away."

Jill sighed with affectionate exasperation. Warren was a lawyer, too, and she knew he'd argue this case until doomsday, but it wouldn't change a thing.

There were good reasons for the separation.

Painful ones—none of which would ever change. Given some technicalities with their property ownership, there were also very impersonal reasons for the delay of those final papers.

"Let it rest, Warren. And while you're at it, I want you to rest, too." She frowned at him to mask her worry. "This was your second heart attack, and that congestive heart failure isn't getting any better. You work too hard and you drink too much. And—no matter what you tell me—I know you're still smoking those cigars."

His expression grew thoughtful. "So I should take it easy."

"Exactly."

"And I shouldn't work such long hours."

"Not if you want to be around to see your first grandchild. Which," she added quickly, "Phil and Sandra are working on at this very moment." At the cagey gleam in Warren's eyes, she knew what was coming before he even started to speak.

"I think I'll take some time off. Tend my flowers. Give the old ticker a rest." He nodded to himself, warming to the idea. "God knows, I've let the place go since Marie died."

Warren lived and breathed the law. His office lights burned late into the night and he was there every morning by eight. The likelihood of him staying away for even a day was nearly impossible to imagine. Unless…

"And of course, I'll need someone to cover the office. For a while, that is. Someone who knows the practice inside and out. Someone who can relate to the fine people here in Blackberry Hill. Someone who—"

"So you're going to ask Grant to come back." The weight of the past settled heavily on her shoulders. "Doesn't his brother need him?"

"Phil covered our office in Kendrick for years before Grant joined him last fall." He shrugged. "I'm sure he can manage a while longer."

"But Grant must have a personal caseload there, now. He's probably very busy."

"It's only two hours away. If he needs to, he can commute to his active cases there."

"But—"

"I'm sure he won't mind coming back here for a few months. Not when his dad is so ill and all…then you wouldn't have to stop by my place every day to check on things." Warren's glance cut toward the bags hanging from the IV pole by his bed. "Of course, if you think I'm ready for discharge, then I probably wouldn't be needing any help…" His voice trailed off, tinged with a hint of hopefulness.

"You are such a stinker," Jill shot back, hiding a smile. "If you're bargaining for a quicker discharge, the answer is no. That infection was a doozy, and you've still got eight more days of IV antibiotics.

After that, you'll need a week or so of rehab to build your strength."

Harumph. Warren settled back against his pillow and regarded her through narrowed eyes. "You and Grant *deserve* each other."

She laughed as she picked up the clipboard on the bedside table. "There, Warren, is where you are totally wrong."

AFTER FINISHING HER rounds at Blackberry Hill Memorial, Jill crunched through the snow in the staff parking lot, thankful for her heavy down jacket and warm boots. Snowflakes swirled beneath the security lights overhead, glittering like crystals against the black sky.

You and Grant deserve each other. Despite all of his contacts in this small town, Warren really didn't have a clue what had happened to his son's marriage. Either that, or he thought an affair—especially an affair with a client—was not a big deal.

With one mittened hand, she swept away the snow on the driver's side window of her Sable station wagon. Beneath the snow she felt a thick cobblestone layer of ice.

"Wind chill of minus-forty tonight. Wind's going to get up to thirty miles an hour, I hear," Grace Fisher called out from her own car another row over. The stocky older woman, director of nursing at the hospital, waved her ice scraper. "Need this?"

"Got one—but thanks." Jill slapped her mittens together to knock the snow off, then slid behind the wheel of her car to start the motor. Retrieving her own scraper, she got out again and started on the windshield. "I'll bet you aren't going to miss these north-woods winters when you retire."

Grace laughed. "If I'm not on some southern beach, I'll at least stay by my fire with a good book."

Jill waved goodbye to her as Grace drove away, then bent over the hood and continued chipping at the ice, her cheeks and fingers already numb.

As soon as she cleared most of the windshield, she climbed back into the car and wrapped her arms around herself, shivering. She wished she had one of those remote car starters so it could have been warm and ready for her.

She drove out of the staff parking lot and took a left, heading down Main through the center of town.

Snow glistened beneath the street lamps, splashed with color where it reflected the neon lights of businesses along the three-block downtown area. In the summer, the shops bustled with the thousands of vacationers who swarmed to the beautiful lake district. Now, many of the upscale shops were closed until May, giving the street a rather melancholy air.

She passed the drugstore and the grocery store,

both on the edge of town, then drove out into the darkness to Bitter Hollow Road, a narrow gravel lane a few miles past the last street lamps. Without the moon and stars overhead the darkness seemed impenetrable....

Until she rounded the last turn and found the lights blazing at Warren's house.

Strange. He lived here alone. She certainly hadn't left on the lights when she'd last stopped by to water the plants.

Fumbling for her cell phone, she slowed her car to a crawl then stopped by the mailbox at the end of the driveway.

The wind was picking up, buffeting clouds of snow beneath the faint light of the single security lamp at the peak of the garage.

She squinted through the falling snow, trying to make out the dark shape parked next to the garage and partially hidden by a stand of pines.

A vehicle, certainly...possibly an SUV, but Warren hadn't said anything about anyone else coming out here.

An intruder...?

With the press of a speed-dial button she called Sheriff Randy Johnson's office before turning up the heater to ward off the chill.

Five minutes stretched to ten, then fifteen.

At six o'clock, faint pinpoints of light appeared

through the increasing snowfall, then drew up behind her. The sheriff briefly flashed the wigwag lights on the front grill of his car to identify himself. He appeared at her door a moment later.

She rolled down her window and flinched as a blast of icy wind hit her. "Thanks for coming out."

"No problem, Doc." Middle-aged and burly, the sheriff had always reminded her of a towering, congenial bear—one that could overpower just about anyone who dared challenge it. He squinted toward the house and garage. "Seen anyone?"

"No…but people inside the house wouldn't know I'm here. I turned off my lights as soon as I stopped."

He nodded his approval. "You were smart not to go barging in. For years, I've been telling Warren he should move closer to town. Even with a security system, this is way too isolated for the old guy."

"I'm supposed to be taking care of his plants," she said through chattering teeth.

"My deputy and I will check this out. If you want to go on home, that would be just fine. I'll give you a call in a bit…or we can just stop up at your place."

Imagining that he wanted her out of the way in case of trouble, she hesitated, then waved goodbye. She shifted her car into Reverse, backed carefully around the patrol car and headed slowly up the two miles to her own home on Bitter Creek Road.

The Sable bucked through the drifts. She nearly

buried it at the low spot where the bridge crossed the creek, but then the spinning tires gained purchase against the gravel beneath the snow and lurched forward. Jill exhaled in relief as she made it up into the timber, where the pines and winter-bare undergrowth of the forest blocked the drifting snow.

At the top of Chapel Hill, the trees gave way to a small clearing and the two-and-a-half-story, red-brick Victorian she and Grant had bought last summer. Back when they'd still imagined filling it with a half-dozen children someday.

Back when she'd still believed in her own fairy-tale ending. After growing up poor raised by her single mother, the house had seemed like a dream come true.

By day, the fanciful cupolas and explosion of gingerbread trim at every edge held their own drab charm. The paint was faded and curling, some of the pieces missing or sagging, but it was still possible to envision what it could become.

Though at night, the house loomed dark and forbidding, its narrow spires rising like daggers through the blowing snow, its windows black and empty.

She parked the car in the garage and scurried across the yard to the broad wraparound porch.

With cold fingers she fumbled her key into the front door lock, then let herself inside and flipped on the vestibule lights with a sigh of relief.

After tapping in her security code on the panel

next to the front closet, she bumped the thermostat up to sixty-five and shucked off her boots and coat.

At the sound of something thundering down the curving, open staircase ahead, she grinned and crouched down. "Hey, Badger!"

Twenty pounds of sinuous fur launched out of the shadows and into her arms, nearly knocking her flat. "Pretty kitty," she crooned, staggering upright with the cat slung over her shoulder. "Weird, but pretty. Have you been a good boy?"

On her way to the kitchen she flipped on the lights in the parlor, where the plants were all still upright in their pots.

And in the library, where she noticed with some relief that the flower arrangement on the coffee table—courtesy of her office nurse, in honor of Jill's thirty-third birthday last week—was still arranged properly in its vase.

"Wow," she murmured, pulling the cat away from her shoulder to look into his face. "Apparently you were still tired from the *last* time I left."

He gave her a baleful look and wiggled until she put him on the floor, then stalked over to his empty food dish and lashed his plume of a tail, clearly put out by the delay.

She took a can of his favorite cat food from the cupboard and stirred in some dry kitty kibble, filled his water dish—from which he would drink *only* if it was full—then reopened the fridge and studied the contents.

Once upon a time, there'd been a hearty stock of provisions in there for the dinners she and Grant had prepared together. Now, the thought of cooking just made her tired. Straightening, she foraged in the freezer for a low-fat packaged dinner and tossed the first one she found into the microwave without bothering to read the label.

A chill swept through the kitchen, so heavy with sadness that she spun around, half expecting to see an apparition standing behind her.

No one was there. Nothing stirred, except the languid lashing of Badger's tail as he chowed down on his dinner.

You're imagining things again.

The security system was new, state of the art, and the house was surely secure. Still, uneasy, she slowly retraced her steps and cautiously peered into the library.

The old chandelier suspended from the pressed-tin ceiling bathed the center of the room in soft light, but left the corners in darkness. She sensed nothing amiss.

Reassured, she laughed at her overactive imagination as she moved to the parlor and rested a hand on the heavy, carved mahogany trim of the archway. Here, too, the soft light of an antique chandelier shadowed the nooks and crannies.

Though the house had been sold unfurnished, she and Grant had found some delightful old pieces up in the attic. A turn-of-the-century sewing machine with cast-iron filigree legs. An old, painted fern pedestal, which she'd refinished to its original deep-oak beauty. A warped rocking chair that—after a trip to a furniture repair shop—now fit nicely at the bay window overlooking the side garden.

They'd put all of the original pieces they'd found into this room, and then she'd added an old, towering secretary, intricately carved, and a lovely old oriental rug in deep jewel tones.

She stilled. When had she moved the rocker to the room's front windows?

Her heart skipped a beat as she stared at it.

Almost imperceptibly, it appeared to be *moving*…as in those final, slow moments after someone has gotten up and walked away.

You really need more sleep. Next, you'll be seeing apparitions in the hallway, and bogeymen in your closet.

It was only the wind, of course. Drafts found their way into the old house whenever the wind blew outside.

A faint sound echoed down the shotgun hallway leading to the front entry. She looked down, surprised to see her hands clenched.

It's only my imagination.

Then again, it might be Sheriff Johnson, here to give her a logical explanation for the lights at Warren's house.

She strode to the front door, already forming an apology when she pulled it open.

"I suppose it was n-nothing—" She stammered to a halt, her hand at her throat, and stared into the face of the man who'd sworn he'd never set foot on Chapel Hill again.

Snow glistened on the broad shoulders of his black wool coat. Clung to the deep waves of his windblown blond hair. His eyes met hers—stormy, compelling, still capable of sending a shiver through her that had nothing to do with the bitter wind swirling past him into the house.

"New approach, I take it. Intimidation by the law," he said, his gravelly voice even deeper from the cold. "You could have just called the house, Jill. Saved the sheriff a trip out here on a night like this."

It took her a moment to find her voice. "I—I saw your father an hour ago. He didn't say you were here, so I had no idea. I thought someone might be ransacking the place."

"I wasn't, and I'll be there for some time. Just thought you should know." Grant turned to go, then looked over his shoulder. "Your home phone's out of order, by the way…and you didn't answer your cell. That's the reason I had to come up here."

The cold, flat expression in his eyes chilled her. "I…must have left it in the car."

He crossed the porch in three strides, descended the steps and disappeared. A moment later he was back with her cell phone.

"I still remember the key code to your car door," he said. "I thought you'd better have this."

She gratefully accepted it, then stood aside. "Would you like a cup of coffee?"

For one brief moment, she saw the old pain and anger reflected in his eyes. "That would be a big mistake. I don't think either one of us wants to go there again. Ever."

"You're right." She stood at the open door and watched him walk away. A few minutes later, she saw a pair of headlights swing around out by the garage. Red taillights disappeared into the snowy darkness.

And he was gone.

Jill closed the door, shoved the dead bolt home and leaned her forehead against the leaded glass insert in the door.

Separation had been the right thing. Their divorce was inevitable, and she didn't want him back. Yet a part of her missed the togetherness. The tenderness. The warmth of another person to snuggle against.

And, if she were honest, she missed the incredible passion she'd never felt with anyone but him.

But she and Grant had grown into two very different people over the years, with different goals, different priorities. Their love had faded…then ended in bitterness and accusations. And she needed a person she could trust, not a man who considered other women free game.

Badger sauntered down the hall and wound around her ankles, purring loudly.

"Guess it's just you and me," she murmured. "At least you're honest."

Picking up the cat, she headed back to the kitchen…and felt the aching loneliness of the house close in around her.

CHAPTER TWO

FROM WHAT SHE could see, retirement was going to be a taste of hell.

Grace flipped through the pages of her kitchen calendar and counted the months. Seven… eight…nine…

In ten months she'd turn sixty-seven. Once, she'd considered celebrating with a bonfire of her sturdy white shoes and the wardrobe of uniforms and lab coats that hung in her closet. Now, she couldn't imagine taking that final walk out the hospital's front door.

What did people do, once they didn't have a daily destination? Didn't have a busy schedule, or staff who counted on their competence and vision to make everything run smoothly?

Without the adrenaline rush of emergencies, the need to think fast, she could imagine her heart slowing down like an old, forgotten windup toy.

Cradling a cup of apricot tea, her gaze drifted to the refrigerator door festooned with photographs.

Newspaper clippings. Wedding and baby announcements—remnants of her decades as a foster parent.

Once, her kitchen had bustled with three or four youngsters at a time; eating hurried breakfasts, making sack lunches, hurrying off to school or sports practice. There'd been crayon pictures taped to that refrigerator, along with reports cards and notices of parent-teacher conferences.

Once, she'd been needed here at home as much as she was still needed at the hospital, but soon this last chapter of her life would end, too, leaving her…with nothing.

Snorting aloud at her self-pity, she grabbed the file folder of cruise brochures propped behind the coffeemaker on the counter and took her tea into the living room.

Old people took trips. Saw the things they'd never had time to see when their families were young and careers were going full swing. It wouldn't be so bad, finally getting to see Europe. Nova Scotia. Oregon.

For years, she'd heard people talk about Banff, too, and before she died she *definitely* had to go see those beautiful lakes up there, that were—supposedly—like lovely pots of paints, in shades of emerald and sapphire.

Life would soon be very peaceful. Quiet. And blast it, she was going to enjoy every minute.

The cordless phone rang on the end table next to

her. Her heartbeat picked up when she read *Blackberry Hill Memorial* on the caller ID.

Marcia Larsen was the nurse in charge tonight. Highly competent, she wouldn't be contacting Grace unless third-shift staff had called in sick…or there was a major emergency.

But it wasn't Marcia's voice on the line when Grace picked up.

"Um…I'm real sorry to bother you, Ms. Fisher," stammered Beth, the receptionist. She lowered her voice, and Grace imagined that the girl was cupping a hand over the receiver. "There's…um…someone here to see you. She wants directions to your *home*."

"You know the policy, Beth. We never give out phone numbers or addresses."

"Of course. But…" In the background, Grace could hear raised, angry voices, and then Beth came back on the line. "She says her name is Ashley, and that she's your niece. She…um…has a teenage son with her who isn't very happy with her right now. I already notified security…but should I call the police?"

Grace tossed the brochures aside, launched out of her chair and headed for the coat closet. "Is the boy's name Ross?"

"Yes, ma'am." Beth sounded worried.

"They're my relatives, but they might have trouble finding my house in the dark. Tell them to calm down, and I'll be there in ten minutes."

Remembering Ashley's volatile temper and her great-nephew's rebellious nature, Grace made it to the hospital in eight minutes, despite the six inches of snow already on the ground and the deepening drift at the corner of Maine and Oak.

Instead of braving the staff parking lot, where the wind had piled snow into dunes near the building, she pulled up into the crescent drive at the front.

Inside, she stamped the snow from her boots, shrugged out of her coat and gave Beth a nod. "Quieter, now?"

The girl tipped her head toward the waiting area. "I brought the woman some coffee, and gave her son a Coke," she said. "Are they *really* relatives of yours? I mean—well—" She blushed.

"Yes, they are," Grace said, frowning. At twenty-two, Beth brought fresh enthusiasm to the job, but she was also prone to being a bit too personal. "I'll take them back to my house once we get things settled down."

Beth's blush deepened. "Yes, ma'am."

"Thanks for calling. I imagine the trip was stressful for them, coming all this way in such bad weather." Grace smiled at her, then headed for the corner of the waiting room where Ross had pulled a chair up in front of the TV. Only the top of his black, curly hair showed over the backrest.

Ashley sat on the edge of a chair near him, her

hands knotted in her lap and her eyes revealing both her tension and exhaustion. She looked up as Grace drew closer, clearly relieved.

"Aunt Grace—I'm *sooo* happy to see you!" She stood and hurried over for a quick hug, then a much longer, second embrace. "I never expected all this snow. The roads were so slick—and the tires on my friend's car aren't all that great. We nearly went in the ditch *twice*."

"It's good to see you again, honey." Grace rested her hands on the younger woman's shoulders and took a half step back to look at her. She had to be twenty-nine by now, but deep lines bracketed her mouth and fanned from the corners of her eyes. She looked forty, and from the stiffness in her spine she was here with news that wasn't good.

Ross twisted around and glared at his mother, then slumped back down and continued watching the sitcom on television.

"Please—can we talk over there?" Ashley pleaded, motioning to a far corner. "I-it's important."

Ross slumped farther down in his seat and cursed under his breath. "Like I don't know everything you're gonna say?"

Ashley's eyes filled with tears. "Please. He's just upset right now, and so am I. It's not what you think."

But Grace already had a pretty good idea, as she led Ashley over to a sofa and loveseat arranged for greater privacy. The girl had led a troubled life, starting with her own rebelliousness at school and a pregnancy at fourteen, then the loss of both parents the year after she graduated from high school.

Ashley seemed to melt into the soft cushions of the loveseat as she stared down at her tightly clasped hands. "We were doing okay, Ross and me. I've held a good job as a teacher's assistant, and I've been going to night school. By summer I'll be done with a whole year of college credits. But then…" Her eyes filled with renewed tears. "Ross started cutting class, and he got in some other trouble at school. He got suspended twice this year. The county says it will file charges against *me* if I don't make sure that he goes to school every day. But I'm working, and going to school…"

"So he's home alone."

"He's got a key," Ashley snapped. Her gaze met Grace's for a split second, then dropped back to her hands. She lowered her voice to a ragged whisper. "It isn't good, I know. He's only a sophomore, and he's already got friends who've dropped out. Friends who…use."

"Sounds like a bad situation." Grace thought back to some of the troubled teenagers she'd taken in over the years. She'd been younger then, able to cope and keep up, but some of those kids had been a full-time job unto themselves. Even so, the drug scene hadn't yet swept into this part of the world.

"I can't be at work and school, and know where he is every minute. He's getting an attitude like his daddy had, the *just-try-and-make-me* sort of sneer teachers hate. And…" She shifted uncomfortably. "He and his buddy were caught shoplifting in December."

"Oh, dear." Grace glanced over at the boy slouched in the chair. He was probably a good five foot nine already, much taller and heavier than his diminutive mother.

"A caseworker got involved," Ashley added hastily. "Ross isn't being sent away. Not this time. But if he messes up again, the judge will send him to a detention center. He's only got one more chance, and I'm scared he's gonna blow it."

Grace gave one fleeting thought to those travel brochures on the coffee table back home, then dismissed them without regret. "If you need money, I do have some put by."

A man in his early thirties appeared at the entryway of the hospital, jingled a set of keys and fixed Ashley with an impatient look.

She nodded to him, then turned back to Grace. "I don't want your money. Come this fall, I should have some student loans set up—me and Ross will be fine."

"Then…"

"I won't even have him by then, if he screws up any more. I need to get him out of Chicago, away from his friends—until the end of this school year."

Ashley leaned forward and took one of Grace's hands into both of her own. "Please. Will you take my son?"

"PRETTY SLICK, HUH?" Ross slouched on the couch in Grace's living room, his mouth twisted in a sneer. "Five-minute intro, and you're stuck with me."

"Stuck isn't the word I would use. Not at all." Grace propped her elbows on the armrests of her recliner and steepled her fingertips under her jaw.

"Like you really wanted to find yourself saddled with a kid you barely know." He turned his head to look disdainfully at her from the pile of crocheted pillows. "I bet you woke up this morning thinking, 'Geez, I wish I had a fifteen-year-old hanging around. For *months*.'"

"It honestly hadn't crossed my mind. But, that doesn't mean you aren't welcome—or that I don't look forward to getting to know you better."

"Ri-i-ight." He drew out the sarcasm.

"I still think your mother and her...friend should have stayed overnight. Chicago is over six hours away in good weather. Tonight, it might take twice as long."

"Tony owns a bar. He'd never miss being there on a weekend. And Mom wouldn't miss her tips."

Surprised, Grace cocked her head. "She said she works as an assistant teacher."

"Part-time. Nights Thursday through Saturday,

she tends bar and hangs out with Tony. She usually turns up at home on Sunday."

So Ross was unsupervised on weekends. Not a good thing, for a boy his age. Especially one who'd already been in trouble.

"First thing, we'll have to get you enrolled in school," Grace said briskly. His jaw stiffened, and despite his bravado, she knew it had to be scary, thinking about walking into a strange school mid-year. A place where he knew no one at all. "I remember there used to be quite a few families coming or going over winter vacation, so you probably won't be the only new face."

"Whatever."

"Your mother," she added with a smile, "must have been pretty sure this would all work out. She said she'd already requested that your school records be sent up here."

He snorted. "If you'd said no, she probably would've just taken off. You never had a choice." He raised a brow. "She and ole Tony had it figured out before they ever left home."

Grace bit the inside of her cheek to hold back a tart reply. Had Ashley been that cunning? As an example to her son, it would be terrible. As an example of her love for him, it was even worse. He was young enough that it had to hurt. Deeply.

"I think it's good that you're here," Grace said

simply. "So tell me, how much trouble were you in, back in Chicago?"

"What—you gonna try to send me back?"

Grace stood and moved an armchair next to the sofa, where she would be in his direct line of vision. "No, I'm going to enjoy your company. This place used to be a madhouse, with all the kids who grew up here. And now, it's way too quiet."

She picked up a tapestry bag of knitting she'd left by the sofa and pulled out a pair of needles and a ball of soft, navy-blue mohair yarn. After casting on a row of stitches, she started knitting.

"This will be a sweater," she said over the soft clicking of her needles. "I could go out to a discount store and buy just any old blue sweater. Maybe pay twenty or thirty dollars. It wouldn't mean anything to me, but it would be cheap and easy."

He stared up at the ceiling with a look of utter boredom.

"Or, I can choose to do something really special. Something that takes a lot of time, a lot of hard work. Sometimes, I'll make a mistake, and I'll have to go back to make it right."

He didn't say anything, though she could tell he was listening.

"But in the end, I have something to be proud of, because of all the love and time that went into it. And in the years to come, I'll remember all the good things that happened in my life while I was working on it."

She finished another few rows, then settled the yarn in her lap. "I can't be your momma, Ross. I'm just your great-aunt. But I promise you that we'll do well together, you and me."

"She *dumped* me here—away from my friends, my school," he said bitterly.

Grace studied him, wishing she could give him the comfort and reassurance he needed. He was fifteen, though, not five—on that cusp of youth between childhood and independence where one had to tread softly.

"You've been up here twice? Three times? Only for brief visits, though." She dropped her gaze back to her knitting and started another row. "I suppose we should be upfront with each other, so there aren't any misunderstandings. As with all the other kids I've raised, I expect you to work hard in school, to keep my curfews and pitch in. I won't tolerate drugs, alcohol or smoking. I expect simple respect, and that's what I'll give you, along with a home as long as you need it."

She looked up at him over her half-glasses. "Now, you tell me your feelings about all of this. Fair enough?"

He levered himself off the sofa and grabbed for his duffel bag—surely not big enough to hold much. For a moment he seemed ready to flee, then he sagged back down, dropped his forearms on his thighs and bowed his head. "I got no choice, do I," he said flatly.

He didn't, unless he chose to run...and that could only lead to more trouble. Grace said a quick, silent prayer for the right words. "Honey, your mom is my niece. That makes me your flesh and blood. I *care* about you. Let's do our best, here, all right? Summer will be here before you know it. In the meantime, maybe you can consider this a bit of a vacation...an *adventure,* in the most beautiful place on earth."

He glanced up at her, and for just a moment she saw beyond his tough shell.

"Have you ever been snowmobiling? Ice fishing? Cross-country or downhill skiing?" Grace mentally catalogued every person she knew in town who could help her out. "Fly fishing? Canoeing?"

"You do all that?" he sneered.

"Cross-country, but my bones are a little too stiff for downhill. Fishing. As for snowmobiling, I know lots of people who are into it, big time."

He stood up and shouldered his duffel bag. "Where do I sleep?"

Grace set aside her knitting, crossed the living room and opened the door leading to the second floor. "Either room up there. You're welcome to re-arrange the furniture any way you'd like, and I'll bring up some linens in just a few minutes." She glanced at her watch. "Are you hungry? Do you want something before you turn in?"

He jerked his head *no,* and tromped up the stairs.

Grace sighed. She'd had many teenagers under her wing. Emotionally damaged, surly, some of them had been homeless or had come from abusive situations, and most of them had chafed against the restrictions of a disciplined household. They'd all come around, with love and patience.

But she'd been much younger then. She'd had the energy and the determination to help those children the best she could, and had sent them out into the world with much greater chance of success.

Now, she felt old. Tired. With the aches of arthritis keeping her awake at night, how was she going to keep up this time? But there was no way she could refuse.

Ross and Ashley needed her, and she was going to make sure she didn't fail them.

CHAPTER THREE

"I CAN'T HELP it, Warren. You're stuck here—with me." Grace frowned at him over her half-glasses. "Just be glad your infection hasn't spread past the surgical site. If all your cronies had to wear gowns, slippers and masks in here, you'd probably have a lot less company. This way, it's just the person changing your dressings who has to gown up."

"Seven more days," Warren grumbled, glaring at the IV pole looming above his bed. "I could be in Florida golfing."

"Or you could be six feet under." Grace double-checked the bag of vancomycin she'd brought in, then hung it with the bag of saline and started the dose. "Not long ago, an antibiotic-resistant staph infection like this one would have killed you."

"No one ever accused you of tact, Gracey."

"I've got *plenty* of tact, Bugs." She grinned. He'd always hated that nickname. Probably hoped he'd left it behind in grade school, when he gave Billy Alderson a black eye. "I just know it doesn't work with you."

Warren snorted.

"But I've got some good news for you—I saw your son talking to Dr. Jill out in the hall, just a few minutes ago. It must be wonderful to have him back, isn't it?"

"Oh, yeah. And it's good to see you. Are you my nurse this shift?"

"Just until Marcia gets here. She had some car trouble."

"Stop back again, would you? It's nice…just talking about old times."

The past couple of days had been more hectic than usual, with a spate of mid-winter injuries and illnesses—influenza, broken legs and ankles from winter sports, bronchitis and pneumonias—and until today she hadn't given him more than a quick greeting.

The loneliness in his eyes touched her heart. "Of course I will."

Grant knocked lightly and walked in, following Dr. Jill. From the strained expression on Jill's face and the rigid set of Grant's shoulders it was all too clear that they still barely tolerated each other's presence.

It was such a shame. Jill was one of her closest friends in the hospital and her ex-husband was still Grace's lawyer—a fine and caring man. How could things have gone so wrong between them?

Grace took one last look at the rate on the IV pump and started for the door to give them privacy.

"How's he doing today?" Jill asked, stopping Grace.

It was a question intended to keep her there—perhaps as a buffer—because every last detail of Warren's day was clearly documented in the interdisciplinary notes section of his chart.

"Quite well," Grace murmured. "His vitals have been normal for the past twenty-four hours. I'd like you to take a look at his IV site, though. I think we'll need to restart it sooner than scheduled."

Jill moved to the bed and smiled in greeting, then inspected his arm. "She's right, Warren. Vanco is hard on the veins. We'll have to change your IV at least twice before you're done."

Warren scowled. "Do whatever you damn well please and then leave me alone."

"Dad—"

"It's okay," Jill said, sparing Grant a chilly glance and then turning her attention back to Warren. "No one likes being here. Right?"

He fixed his stony gaze on the wall just over her head.

The similarity between Grant, Jill and Warren almost made Grace smile. They were strong, intelligent people—and all of them had definite opinions. When the three got together, sparks flew.

Grace silently commiserated with Jill above the patient's head, then gathered her tray of supplies and slipped out the door.

GRANT LEANED BACK in his father's ancient, leather-upholstered desk chair and smiled. "So you're saying you want to rewrite your will again, Mr. Walthan?"

Hal pursed his lips and studied the ceiling, apparently deep in thought. "Mebbe."

"You're not sure."

"I'm thinking about it. My fool grandson…" The old man's heavy neck wattle jiggled as he shook his head in disgust. *"Tattoos."*

"Tattoos." Grant drummed a forefinger on the thick client folder he'd pulled. It held at least four other versions of the man's will, all drafted within the past year, all disinheriting one family member or another. "You want to disinherit him because he got tattoos? They're pretty common these days."

"He's got snakes crawlin' up one arm. A black widow spider crawling down the other." Hal drew his bushy white eyebrows together. "Not the kind of appearance the town expects of a Walthan."

"Pretty soon you're going to run out of relatives. And, if it appears you've been capricious, unduly influenced by anyone or have made some…unusual…decisions, there could be family members who try to contest."

"Your job is to make sure that can't happen." The elderly pharmacist set his jaw. "Then just let 'em try."

Grant jotted a few more notes on the legal pad in

front of him. "I'll write up a new draft, then. When you come back in, I'll ask you to go over each of your wishes—with a witness present—and I'll videotape proof that you appeared to be of sound mind. I'll also ask you for a handwritten summary."

Hal nodded decisively. "You're a good man. Thorough. Never should have left town, if you ask me."

Over the past week, a cadre of the old-timers had trooped into the office, one after another.

Grant had the distinct feeling that a campaign was afoot, after three had given him marital advice, two had told him that he'd been negligent in leaving his father's practice last fall, and every last one of them had made sly, oblique comments about Doc Jill Edwards being far too pretty to—as crotchety old Leo Crupper had put it—"wither on the vine."

Grant steeled himself for the inevitable pep talk from Hal. And sure enough, the old guy hesitated at the door and turned back, one gray brow raised.

"The missus doing well?"

"Fine. Just fine." At least, Grant thought so. He hadn't seen her for a week now, except for the occasional glimpse of her Sable.

He had a feeling Jill wanted to avoid him just as much as he wanted to avoid her.

Hal fixed him with a piercing look. "You aren't getting any younger."

Well, at least he took a different approach from

Warren's other cronies. Who'd probably, now that Grant thought about it, been sent by Warren himself.

"None of us are," Grant replied.

"You got no kids," Hal said bluntly. "No grand-kids for Warren, and there'll be none for you either, down the road, if you wait too long."

Remembering how many grandkids Hal had already disinherited—and then added back into his will—Grant just smiled. "They are a joy, aren't they? Every last one of them. No matter how unique."

"Er…exactly," Hal gave him a narrow look, then stood in the doorway as he shouldered into his coat. "When should I come back?"

Grant flipped the page on the planner lying open on the desk. "Tomorrow's Friday, and I need to take off early. How about next Tuesday. Another ten o'clock?"

"Good enough." He clenched his fingers into the thick crown of his beaver-fur hat. "How's Warren?"

"Much better. He got his IV out yesterday and has started rehab. He'll be home in a week or two, and not a minute too soon. He's been climbing the walls."

"Bet he has. Man never misses a day on the golf course from Easter 'til Thanksgiving, barring snow. He isn't one to sit around."

"Well…he's agreed to take it easy for a few months, if I stay to help out."

"You're a good son, coming back like this to take his place. A real good son."

Grant rounded the desk and walked him to the front door, then flipped the Open sign in the door to Closed as Hal headed down the sidewalk toward Waltham Drug.

At the open doorway Grant took a deep breath of icy, pine-scented air. Thankful, he admitted to himself, that he'd had a reason to come back home to Blackberry Hill for a while.

A couple of blocks down the street, on the corner of Birch and Main, he could see the front corner of Jill's office, and that brought back all the reasons why he shouldn't have.

Clean breaks were the best. Especially when there was no hope of ever changing the past, and no wish to create a future.

Yet he'd run into Jill almost every day at the hospital when he'd stopped to visit Dad.

The irony was that apparently they'd both been changing their schedules to avoid each other—and for once in their lives, they had been in perfect harmony.

But in a few weeks Dad would be on his feet and out of the hospital, and then there'd be no need to intrude on Jill's territory. And that would make life a heck of a lot easier.

PROCLAIMING THAT HE was bored silly on the Skilled Care unit of the hospital, Warren had called the law office at eleven o'clock, noon, one o'clock, and then—apparently he'd been napping—not until almost four.

Grant glanced at the caller ID, amused, as he tapped the speaker button. "Hey, Dad."

Warren sucked in a sharp breath. "There's not a client with you?"

"Your friend Hal left a few minutes ago." Swiveling his chair, Grant looked out the window at the early winter darkness. "Even if there was, I'd guess most people around here know that you and I are related. I've been calling you 'Dad' since I was in diapers."

"Doesn't sound professional."

Grant had visited Warren every day when he was in the ICU in Green Bay, and had figured he would settle down once he was transferred back to Blackberry Hill. But with each passing day it was becoming more obvious that he viewed his ongoing hospitalization as a form of incarceration.

"How are you feeling?"

"Never better."

"Not tired at all? The surgeon in Green Bay said—"

"The doc is nuts. I'm fine as frog hair and going stir-crazy in this place. Let me tell you, the day I decide to retire is the day you'll have to lock me away."

"Dad, how long has it been since you took a vacation—really went somewhere and did something fun?"

During the long silence they both remembered Marie Edwards's unexpected death at fifty-five from an aneurysm. Three years ago.

Grant had been working at a prestigious firm in Chicago, but Warren had been so devastated over the loss of his wife that Grant and Jill had come home to help him cope with his practice and his grief.

After Warren's subsequent heart attack, the intended few months had somehow evolved into several years…with Jill working at an established family practice in town and Grant busy at the Edwards Law Office.

The purchase of a house had signified a commitment to stay for good.

One more painful irony, among the many.

"…so maybe I will." Warren cleared his throat. "What do you think?"

Grant shook himself out of his memories. "About what?"

"I should call him. Haven't been down to see him since he and your Aunt Jane built their new house. I expect we could get in a little golf."

Grant blinked. Uncle Fred and Aunt Jane? *Florida?*

"That is, if you don't mind staying on for a while longer." The hopefulness in Warren's voice faded as he added, "But I shouldn't even ask. You'd probably rather move ahead with your own career, and with my secretary gone, the job is damned inconvenient. Doretta sure picked a bad time to retire."

"I've already planned on staying for several more months, anyway. I don't mind working alone." Grant smiled to himself as he recalled Dad's confrontational relationship with his strong-minded secretary of the past thirty years. "It would do you a world of good to get away for a while. And when you get back, you can hire a nice paralegal."

At a tentative knock on his office door, Grant glanced at his wristwatch. Five o'clock. He'd turned the door sign to Closed when Hal left, which accounted for the knock. "I've got to hang up, someone's at the door."

Grant dropped the phone back into its cradle and rounded the desk. Out in the waiting area, he pinned a welcoming smile on his face as he opened the front door.

And looked down into the lovely face of the woman who'd helped destroy his life.

JILL LINGERED IN the exam room after her last patient of the day left, dictated her progress note into a recorder then popped out the microcassette and strolled to the front office.

Donna Iverson, her office nurse, looked up from a file drawer and grinned. "For once, you're actually done on time. Amazing."

"It is—especially in the middle of flu season." She put the cassette into an envelope and dropped it into a drawer of the receptionist's desk. "After rounds at the hospital, I'm going home for a long, hot bath and a good book."

Middle-aged and motherly, Donna frowned and shook a finger at her. "You need to get out more. Have some fun. What about that nice assistant manager down at the bank? I swear, if that man isn't interested in you, I'll eat my stethoscope."

The man was a pleasant, earnest sort of guy. He'd certainly be Mr. Dependability…and just the thought made Jill stifle a yawn. "I'm not even divorced yet and, frankly, I can't even imagine dating again. But what about you?"

Donna gave a flustered wave of her hand after she pushed the file drawer shut. "It's not so easy, getting back into the swing of things at my age. My brother Bob and his family are here in town, though. Grandkids. Plenty to keep me busy. But you…"

"I've finally got a practice of my own. The house of my dreams. A very devoted cat."

"You've got one very *weird* cat, and a very big house to ramble around in. You know, my bachelor cousin Irwin lives down in Minocqua, and—"

Laughing, Jill held up a hand. "Stop. I'm sure he's a great guy, but I really don't want to meet *anyone*. Ask me again in about five years."

Loyal to a fault, the nurse had stood staunchly by Jill during the difficult last months of her marriage, and she still spoke Grant's name with a sniff of distaste.

"Well…just keep Irwin in mind. He's great with kids. Has a good job in real estate. And," she added triumphantly, "he's never been married, so you wouldn't be taking on all that extra baggage."

I'd just have all of my own. Jill nodded politely as she shouldered into her red wool pea coat and wrapped a long black scarf around her neck. "You should get going. All of this will be waiting for you tomorrow."

"Just another few minutes." Donna's expression grew somber. "Say hello to Patsy, won't you? Tell her I'll stop in tonight with some new magazines."

"She'll be happy to hear that." Jill pulled on her gloves, wishing she could offer more hope for Donna's neighbor. "She may not be very talkative, though. We had to increase her morphine last night."

Patsy Halliday had been the picture of good health just three months ago at her annual physical, but last month she'd come in with severe headaches. An MRI revealed a fast-growing tumor that the surgeons couldn't completely remove, and soon her three young children would lose their mother.

Life was so terribly unfair.

Jill slung the strap of her purse over her shoulder and went out the back door of the clinic, lost in thought. She barely felt the cold as she started her car and waited for the defroster to melt away the haze on her windshield.

Cases like this one kept her awake at nights; made her rethink every decision a dozen times, and made her pray for miracles when everything on the MRI report and labs told her there was little hope.

Cases like this made her want to live every day to the fullest, because they illustrated with cruel finality just how little control you had over the future.

Yet now she was going home to an empty, cavernous house, with only a demented cat and the whispers of old ghosts to keep her company.

"Quite an exciting life you lead," she muttered to herself as she pulled out of the back parking lot, waited for several cars to pass, then turned north on Main.

The deep tire ruts in the snow grabbed at her tires as she drove slowly enough to keep ample distance between her and the car ahead.

The single stoplight in town turned yellow at her approach and, despite her best intentions, she glanced at the Edwards Law Office on the opposite corner.

She drew in a sharp breath.

Dressed in khaki slacks, a blazer and a shirt open at the throat, Grant was at the open door, talking to a woman who stood with her back to the street.

The woman rested her hand on his forearm for a moment, then stood on her toes to kiss his cheek. She turned and hurried down the steps to an all-too-familiar red, vintage Cobra parked in front.

At the car, she turned back and waved at him, her long, too-bright auburn hair whipping in the wind.

Jill's heart gave an extra, hard thud. *Natalie.*

The old hurt welled up inside her and she sat frozen through the green light until the car behind her honked.

She hadn't wanted to believe the rumors last fall. Even now, perhaps this wasn't what it seemed. But Natalie's advances a moment ago certainly hadn't been rebuffed.

Since Grant had come back to town, he and Jill had carefully tried to avoid each other, but small towns didn't allow for a lot of space. Seeing him again had made her feel a little…wistful. Made her start reviewing the past. Made her second-guess all that had gone wrong.

But those regrets were a waste of time.

Grant could do whatever he liked, with whomever he liked, and it didn't matter one bit. He was a free man.

And seeing the woman who'd destroyed the last hope for their marriage drove that fact home with blinding clarity.

CHAPTER FOUR

JILL PAUSED AT the door of Patsy's hospital room to study the rainbow of crayon drawings taped to the wall, the untidy bouquet of flowers on the bedside table.

Zoe's work, Jill thought sadly. The four-year-old loved to handle the flower arrangements delivered to the room, beaming as she plucked one bloom after another and presented them to her mother.

What was it like, seeing your mommy lying so still in this hospital bed, with the steady snick of an IV pump marking off the seconds?

Patsy's head turned on the pillow, her weary eyes lighting with recognition. Her hand dropped to the white cotton blanket, and a small tape recorder fell from her grasp.

Jill caught it just before it hit the floor.

"Thanks," Patsy whispered. "I'm…trying. So hard. I need…time."

The effort to speak clearly exhausted her, and Jill felt renewed anger at the doctor who'd originally misdiagnosed this poor woman. The HMO system that had refused to cover the tests that might have caught her cancer earlier. And especially, at the callous husband who'd walked out on her right after her diagnosis.

No one deserved to die young.

And no one deserved life more than this young mother of three who, until recently, had operated a day-care program in town and had selflessly reached out to others in need.

Jill fingered the stack of audio cassettes on the bedside table. "Your children will treasure these."

Patsy's gaze veered to the tapes, then back to Jill. "The kids will have my memories…of them when they were small. I want them to know…how much I love them. That I'll love them forever."

"They'll never have any doubt."

"Zoe won't even remember me, really." Patsy winced and fell silent for a moment. "She's so young."

"But she'll have these tapes, with your voice. She'll have photos. Do you have home movies?"

"Some." A faint smile flickered at the corners of her mouth. "I'm always on the other side of the camera, though."

"How about getting some film of you and the kids here—maybe down in the lounge? You could be reading to Zoe, or telling some old stories from when you were young. I'll bet we can get one of the nurses to run the camera."

"K-Kurt got it."

In a divorce that had been far from equitable, if the rumors were true. "Then I'll bring in mine," Jill said briskly. "How about that? I'll bring it in tomorrow, and leave it at the nurse's station with a few extra blank cassettes."

"Not sure I'm ready for prime time," the younger woman said, touching the wisps of her thin hair. But the grateful expression in her eyes spoke volumes.

"There are people who will never be beautiful, no matter how perfect their hair. But you? Your kids will treasure every moment. And once the tapes are transferred onto DVDs, the copies will last forever. Or so I was told," Jill added with a smile, "by the young guy at the electronics store who sold me a DVD/VHS dubbing machine."

"Thank you."

She was so clearly exhausted that Jill glanced at the clock on the wall. "I need to let you get some rest, so you'll be ready when the kids arrive." She picked up the chart at the end of the bed and studied the nurse's notes and lab reports. "You know that you can still request hospice if you change your mind?"

"No. I want home…to be happy for them. Not a place where they watched me…die."

"Hospice can get you back here before that point,

if you still want to," Jill said gently. "They'll help you be comfortable, and they'll help your children deal with all of this."

Yesterday Patsy had refused to even discuss it. Now, she blinked away the moisture in her eyes. "For them, then…if it will help."

"I don't think you'll regret it."

"I could go home and stay for a little while? With this?" She lifted a fragile hand toward the IV pole. "And I…could come here when…when…"

"Everything, just as you wish." Jill put the chart on the window ledge and sat beside Patsy on the bed. She took one of her hands. "The nurses tell me you've been refusing your morphine."

"Makes me too…fuzzy. I need to visit with my kids." She managed another faint grin. "Alison says it makes me sound drunk."

Her nine-year-old daughter probably knew about that kind of behavior all too well, given who her father was. The thought of that jerk—an arrogant, self-righteous dentist who'd had an affair with his hygienist, then abruptly moved to Green Bay and filed for divorce—set Jill's teeth on edge. "But what about your pain control?"

"Okay." Patsy sank deeper into the pillow. Her eyes fluttered shut and her breathing deepened.

Her heart heavy, Jill watched her for a moment, then she picked up the chart and headed for the door.

Even after two years in family medicine, she still found it impossible to accept that a stroke of terrible luck could strike anyone, anytime.

Patsy's husband hadn't asked for shared custody. He hadn't arranged a single visit since he'd walked out.

And soon three young children were going to be left in his care, because their loving mother was going to die.

"HEY, ROSS. GREAT NEWS!" his mom gushed into the phone. She giggled, breaking away from the call to tell Tony to leave her alone, and Ross could just imagine what the guy was doing. Pawing her, probably. Playing vampire at her neck.

Tony's smarmy possessiveness over his mom had made Ross's stomach churn from day one, and he'd so wanted to land a fist right in the creep's smug face. The guy was way older than she was, for one thing. And there was something about him that made Ross's skin crawl.

He started to hang up when she came back on the line breathless and laughing. "Sweetie, you'll never guess! Tony and I are going to Reno—we're getting *married!*"

He froze, unable to speak.

"We're leaving tomorrow on an early flight. It will be so cool! We'll take in some of the shows, and

I hear the food is great. Tony knows of a little chapel where they have real flowers and everything…. Are you still there? Did you hear me?"

Ross mumbled something unintelligible into the receiver.

"Look, I know you're gonna be real disappointed, but it's just me and him going. He got a great deal on tickets and a hotel for two. And," she added after another burst of laughter and the sound of Tony's voice in the background, "it *is* our honeymoon."

"Y-you planned this all along." Ross swallowed hard. "You took me up here so you could go to *Reno?*"

"Of course not, sweetie. It…it just sorta came up. Just last night, in fact. Isn't it exciting?"

Just sort of came up? The week after she'd dumped him in Grace's lap? The false cheerfulness in her voice told him she was lying, which just made it worse. "Yeah, right. Exciting."

"It's still a good thing you're up there with Grace," she added quickly. "Tony's real busy with the bar and all, and…well, you know."

"Yeah."

"I'd think you could at least be happy for me." Her voice took on a petulant edge. "You know how we've struggled."

She'd never noticed that Tony was a real jerk toward Ross. She'd been defensive and even angry when he tried to tell her, because she didn't want to hear it.

In return, Ross had never tried to hide his own disgust. Especially not after he'd seen the bastard coming out of a late-night movie with another woman, though Mom had refused to hear a single word against her latest lover.

A chill settled over Ross as he dropped the receiver into its cradle; a feeling of emptiness so huge that if he'd been a few years younger, he might have just sat and bawled.

Grace had tactfully left the kitchen when Ross answered the phone, and from out in the living room he'd heard the sound of her bustling around. Now, she appeared at the kitchen door. "About ready for school? I'll give you a ride."

"Nah." He grabbed his jacket from the back closet and shouldered on his backpack. She'd offered every day of his first week here, and every day he'd refused. With no school bus service for the town kids he could be dropped off like a grade-schooler or he could get there on his own. No contest, there— even if it meant eight blocks of snow-packed streets through the bitter cold.

"Are you sure?" Biting her lip, she glanced outside. "It's five below and windy this morning. The streets aren't that good, either. People don't even try to ride bikes here this time of year, and I really don't mind—"

"No." Before she could push any further or worse,

ask him about the phone call, he jerked open the back door, unchained his mountain bike and hoisted it down the steps.

He slung a leg over the bike and sped down the long hill toward Main Street without a backward glance. He didn't have to look back to know that Aunt Grace was watching him from the porch, her arms folded across her chest and her brow furrowed with worry.

Her house was small, and she'd probably heard some of the conversation.

The roughly plowed street caught his front tire. He wobbled wildly for a split second, then righted himself and eased into the track of a car. *Great—I might as well break my neck and be done with it.*

As cold as it was in this godforsaken place, he was already so numb he probably wouldn't even feel a thing. The phone call this morning almost made him wish he had the courage to let it happen.

For now, he had a place with Grace. But what about later?

Moving back with Mom would no longer be an option. Though Tony had a creepy way of being nice to his mom while getting her to wait on him, his whole personality changed when she wasn't home. He swore a lot, slammed things around and got his kicks out of trying to be intimidating.

It didn't take any imagination to guess how much he'd dislike having a teenage kid around.

A gust of wind kicked up a blinding cloud of snow at the intersection of Oak and Lake. A dark shape suddenly materialized at his left. *Coming too fast...*

Ross slammed on his brakes and jerked the bike to the right. Skidded sideways. From far away he heard a heavy thud and someone screaming.

For one dizzying moment he felt as if he were weightless, spinning, disoriented. And then the ground rushed up to meet him.

THE HOSPITAL'S ONLY male nurse, Carl Miller, met Grace at the door of the E.R. "He's in Room 3. Dr. Reynolds is with him right now." He tipped his head toward the waiting room. "The girl who hit him is here, too, and her father is on the way. She's pretty upset."

Grace nodded and hurried down the hall, her damp shoes squeaking on the highly polished floor.

A heartbeat after she'd received the call, she'd grabbed her purse and coat without a thought for snow boots, gloves or scarf. Now, with snow melting inside her shoes and her hands tingling, she wrapped her arms around herself and tried to stop shaking. *I never should have let him leave home like that. I should have made him sit down and talk.*

But she knew just how far she would've gotten. She'd had him for over a week now, and still hadn't made it past his sullen anger. He'd been less talkative with each passing day.

At the door of the room she said a silent prayer, then hid her worries behind a bright smile and stepped inside.

A bag of saline hung from the IV pole at the other side of the bed. No ventilator, though. *Thank God.* No frantic rushing to get the boy to surgery. And of the four doctors who had privileges at this hospital and could be on call today, Connor Reynolds and Jill Edwards were the very best.

Dr. Reynolds was bent over the bed with his stethoscope on Ross's bare chest. He straightened at the sound of Grace's squeaky shoes, a reassuring smile on his lean, handsome face. "Ross had a mishap, but he's going to be fine."

"Oh, my Lord," she whispered. She hurried to the other side of the bed and ran her hands gently over Ross's face, then his arms and chest.

The abraded, reddened areas over one cheekbone and his left arm would be deep purple by tomorrow. The sheet, drawn up to his waist, might hide more serious injuries, but so far, she could see no bandaging, no evidence of lacerations. "Are you okay, honey? What happened?"

Ross darted a wary look at her, his cheeks reddening. He closed his eyes and turned away. "Nothing."

Did he expect her to be *angry?* She wanted nothing more than to gather him up in her arms and comfort him.

An impossibility, given the situation and his teenage pride.

Swallowing back her emotions, she gripped the side rail on the gurney. "He says this is *nothing?*" She looked up at Dr. Reynolds. "Tell me."

"We've got a young man here who's been rethinking his idea about biking in the winter. He was very lucky. Deputy Krumvald says the accident happened at an unmarked intersection, and it isn't clear who was there first. The car hit his back tire and sent him about fifteen feet into heavy snow banked up along the street."

"Thank God."

"Still, that snow wasn't exactly a feather pillow—those banks are hard-packed and crusted. He's got some scrapes and bruises, and a light sprain in his left wrist."

"X-rays?"

"He just came back. We took X-rays of the wrist, ran an MRI and some lab work. No sign of internal damage or a concussion, though I suspect he'll be sore for a while. I recommend bandaging the wrist, a cold pack and elevation for a day. After that, just wrap it until it feels comfortable." The doctor smiled. "I think the worst part of this for him was starting that IV."

It had been placed immediately, Grace knew, in case there'd been a fast decompensation of Ross's status. A rush to surgery. Something she dealt with frequently, even in this small hospital.

But now, with Ross lying in this bed, the fact that he was on an IV hit her hard. What if he'd been seriously injured? *What if he'd—*

She struggled to rein in her escalating emotions. "Thank you, Connor."

"I'm glad I was here. So, buddy," he said, resting a hand on Ross's shoulder. "You're one lucky guy. We'll pull the IV and you can go home. Does a day off school sound like a good plan?"

Ross looked up at Connor, then his gaze veered toward Grace for an instant. "I guess."

Carl appeared at the door. "There's a young lady out here who'd like to see Ross," he said in a low voice. "Her father is with her as well. Should I have them come back later?"

Connor shrugged. "I'm done here. If you want to take care of his IV and discharge instructions, he can leave. Ross, do you want to see this gal?"

Tucking the blankets up to his shoulders, Ross shook his head.

"Is this the driver of the car that hit him?" Grace frowned. "I'm not sure we're in a position to talk about liability, yet."

"The deputy was here a while ago to take a statement from Ross, and he got one from her a few minutes ago. She says she's just worried about how Ross is doing."

"Ross?" When he didn't answer, Grace leaned

closer. "If this is a girl from school, you'll end up running into her anyway, so maybe this is best. Just don't discuss any fault issues, ok?"

"I'm not *stupid*."

She bit back the words she would have said if he'd been rude at home, then nodded to Carl. A few minutes later a blond teenager with cornflower-blue eyes and tear-streaked cheeks timidly stepped inside the door.

Her father, a burly, scowling man in his fifties, hovered at her shoulder. "So what's the story, here? Doesn't look too serious."

Connor looked at Grace and raised a brow. She shook her head. They both knew what he was angling for—an admission that Ross was just fine and a quick, tidy resolution—but anyone in the profession knew that some injuries could show up later. Damage that could require long-term physical therapy.

"Well?" the man insisted.

"Daddy, *please*." The girl moved tentatively to Ross's side. "I hope you're all right," she said carefully, with a glance back at her father. She smiled tremulously at Ross. "I'm Mandy Welbourne. I've…um…seen you at school. I think we have third-hour algebra together."

His Adam's apple bobbed as he swallowed and pulled the sheet up higher under his chin. "Uh…maybe."

"If…you need to be out of school awhile, I could bring you your homework."

"Mandy." Her dad gripped her shoulder. "It's time for us to go."

She bit her lower lip, then twisted away from his grasp. "I just want you to know how sorry I am. Really. I didn't see you at all and—"

"Mandy!" Her father glared her into silence then gave Ross a narrowed look. "The idea of someone riding a bicycle on those icy, rutted streets, with the wind kicking up a ground blizzard is incomprehensible. Absolutely *incomprehensible*. My daughter has suffered severe emotional trauma over this little incident."

He guided his daughter out of the room with a firm hand at her back, and Grace could well imagine what the man was going to say to the poor child after they were out of earshot.

Connor seemed to think Ross would be fine, and maybe Ross and Mandy were both at fault for the accident. But if Welbourne thought he could bully a teenage boy into a fast resolution, he'd better think twice.

With Grace in Ross's corner, the man didn't stand a chance.

CHAPTER FIVE

"IF YOU DO that one more time, you're *back in the cage.*" Grant glared up at the rearview mirror and into Sadie's unrepentant brown eyes.

A second later, her pink tongue slurped his right ear and she rested her long nose on his shoulder…then eased a little closer until her head was pressed firmly against his neck.

"I *mean* it."

But it was a hard call which was better: listening to her howls from inside her portable kennel or dealing with her kisses. After the first hour in the car his ears had been ringing and the steady thud of a headache started pounding behind his temple. He'd let her loose in the SUV then, but three Tylenols and another hour later, the painful cadence still hadn't faded. For Sadie, long car rides were an anxious event, and she obviously needed all the reassurance she could get.

"Just another fifteen, twenty minutes, a short stop

at the office and we'll be home." He reached back and gave her a quick rub under the collar. "Not long at all. Then you'll have a big fenced yard, and you can bark at birds all day long."

She slurped at his ear in gratitude, then leaned farther over the back of the seat and plastered her head against the side of his neck, her eyes closed.

Grant sighed. The dog kisses were bad enough. What had to be a hundred pounds of dead weight on his neck and shoulder for the past hour was probably going to send him into physical therapy for life.

"You know," he said as he parked behind the law office in Blackberry Hill, "if you *hadn't* been so hell-bent on barking at birds, you could have stayed with Phil. *He's* the one who thought you were going to be a nice little house dog. Not me."

He reached back and snapped on the leash, then climbed out of the SUV and opened the back door. Sadie lumbered out and shook vigorously, sending a cloud of black fur into the air.

Now the size of a small pony, as a puppy she'd been dropped off at a humane shelter with her littermates. The owner, who'd filled out paperwork on the pups, had apparently had a good idea of what was in store, after his Newfoundland carried on an illicit affair with the sexy Great Dane down the street.

Massive size—and a hell of a lot of hair.

Phil had had a few second thoughts as she grew

and grew...but the barking, which violated a Kendrick city ordinance and resulted in fifty dollar fines every time a neighbor complained, had been the last straw. At two hundred dollars, he'd said she was on "probation."

At three hundred, Phil had advertised her in the newspaper to no avail. Which meant she faced incarceration at the city dog pound and a possible death sentence through no fault of her own.

Grant had been unable to let that happen.

She wandered at the end of the leash, nose to the ground until she did her business, while he debated what to do with her.

Lifting the heavy, recalcitrant dog into that cage sounded like a recipe for disaster—she'd fallen for the lure of dog cookies once, but probably wouldn't be so naive again.

And God only knew what she'd do to the upholstery if she started pining for him again.

During a quick rest stop, he'd walked her and then put her back into the vehicle so he could run to the rest room. She'd shredded his Wisconsin map, destroyed a Thermos and polished off a package of Oreo cookies.

"Okay," he said firmly, lifting her nose so she'd have to look him straight in the eyes. "You can come inside. But no funny business. Promise? Sit. Lie down. That's it."

She promptly sat and swept the snow with her bushy tail.

"Okay, then. Heel!"

She bounded to the end of her leash and eagerly pawed at the back door, nearly jerking him off his feet.

"You, my friend, are going to dog school," he muttered as he unlocked the door. Walking past his dad's office, he entered the smaller one he'd always used, fished a couple of dog treats from the pocket of his ski jacket and settled Sadie in the corner behind his desk.

Where, hopefully, she would stay quietly until he finished the meeting with his client.

Vance Young arrived a few minutes later, still wearing his gas station uniform and smelling of sweat, gasoline and motor oil. His scowl suggested that he was as volatile as the fuels staining his shirt.

Grant led him into the office and waved him toward one of the chairs by the desk, then he picked up the files he'd left by the phone. "I wasn't sure why you wanted to come in today, so I pulled all of these."

A muscle along the side of the man's jaw jerked. "Those damn payments, that's why."

"Payments?"

"Warren said he'd take care of it. Straighten it out. The damn county is after me for back child support, and I sure as hell don't plan to pay."

"Aah." Grant thumbed through the files until he found the correct one. "What's the problem?"

"I said, I don't plan to pay." He spat out each word. "My ex-wife makes as much money as I do. She ain't supporting another family like I am…and she's living in sin with another man, right there with my kids. So what are you gonna do about this?"

"Those factors don't negate your financial responsibility as a father, Vance. Do you pay her alimony?"

"Hell, no."

"That probably could have been terminated, given the circumstances." Grant was beginning to see why the woman had agreed to a divorce…she'd probably hit the ground running at the first opportunity and never looked back. He glanced at the latest court order in the file. "Says here you were to start paying three-hundred-fifty dollars a month almost three years ago. Exactly how far behind are you?"

"Eight grand."

"Kids are expensive, Vance. That translates into a lot of ballet lessons, school fees and soccer equipment. Running shoes. Clothes. Food. A percentage of what keeps a roof over their heads."

"She *got* the damn house." His face reddened. "She got her car. She got the kids."

Either the man was obtuse, or refused to pay attention to reason. "How old is her car?" Grant asked mildly, tapping a forefinger on the desk. "How old is the house?"

Vance's eyes narrowed. Glittered, beneath the heavy folds of his lids. "A '93. Good car. The house, 1960."

"Sooo…she's got repairs and routine maintenance on an old house. Heat. Electricity. Taxes. Repairs on an old car. You know the drill, Vance. I see that you've unsuccessfully petitioned twice now to have your child support substantially lowered. Yet with inflation, she's already getting less."

Vance launched out of his chair and planted his meaty fists on the desk. "Who are you representing here? *I'm* the client."

From the shadows behind his chair, Grant heard Sadie growl—barely audible. "I am representing your best interests. Yes, you can go to court. But it's going to cost you. And when you get there, the judge will take a hard look at your failure to pay. With luck, you'll get a warning and a deadline for catching up. In *full*. If he or she is feeling testy, you could owe penalties, have your wages garnished or even end up in the slammer. I understand that the local paper is now publishing photos in a column called 'Deadbeat Dads,' and if you end up there it could hurt your business."

Vance pounded the desk. "I've got a two-bit lawyer!" he roared. "And I'm supposed to pay her because you people can't do your job?"

"You pay her because you fathered those kids."

Vance started to reach across the desk.

"I really wouldn't do that, if I were you," Grant warned.

"What?" Vance sneered. "You think you—"

Sadie erupted into a frenzy of barking and launched from the shadows to just inches from Vance's face, her massive jaws snapping, and sledgehammer-sized front paws scrabbling at the top of the desk.

Files and loose papers flew.

The desk lamp crashed to the floor.

"I've got her." Grant grabbed at Sadie's collar, but with a cry, Vance stumbled backward, tripped over the chair and half fell to the floor.

He scrambled to his feet and backed toward the door, his hands braced protectively in front of him, palms out. "I won't be back, but I won't forget this, either," he snarled when he reached the door. He reached behind, turned the knob and opened the door wide enough to get out. "If your dad did his job, I wouldn't be in this mess. I'm gonna find a lawyer who knows what he's doing."

After he slipped through the door like a cornered weasel, Sadie whined and licked Grant's ear. *Again.*

"You are a ton of trouble, you know that?" He ruffled her fur and hauled her off the desk, trying to imagine her barreling through his father's house, still filled with so much of his late mother's glass and china frippery. "But maybe you aren't so worthless after all."

Sadie needed a big house. A big yard. An owner who loved dogs but didn't have one right now…and who lived in an isolated area where a canine alarm system might be welcome.

He grinned, just thinking about all the mayhem the dog could cause. "In fact, I think I know someone who needs a dog just like you."

"TELL ME, GRACEY, what's a hot chick like you doing at this hospital on a Friday night?"

"Working. Unlike some people who get to take it easy." Grace jotted Warren's temp down on a slip of paper and shifted her stethoscope into position. "Take a deep breath."

He waited patiently as she finished his vitals. "I'm serious. I remember you in high school—sweetest gal around. Why didn't you ever get married? Settle down and have a family of your own?"

"The longer you stay here, the nosier you get, *Bugs*." His words touched a nerve, and she couldn't quite temper the sharpness in her voice. "I've done exactly what I wanted to do. I had a passel of foster kids to raise, a job I love."

"Aw, Grace…I didn't mean to pry." His eyes were troubled. "Maybe I'm thinking about the past too much these days, lying here. It isn't easy, getting older and being alone."

Exactly her own thoughts, though their situations

were far different. He'd had a lifetime with Marie—anyone could've seen how happy they were together. And she'd just had…dreams.

"It must be hard for you, with Marie gone. I'm sorry."

"It's hell," he muttered. "But at least I had almost forty great years. Now I look at my son and his wife, and I could spit nails. How can they throw away something so good?"

This evening, Grant had stopped in early to see his dad. Jill had tactfully gone to check on her other inpatients first, then visited Warren after his son was gone.

"Maybe it wasn't that good for them," Grace said as she draped the stethoscope around her neck and gathered her things. "You have to admit they don't seem happy together."

"In my day, people worked things out. Stuck together through everything, no matter what," Warren grumbled. He poked at the applesauce a nurse's aide had brought him a few minutes ago, then shoved it away in disgust.

"But sometimes, that wasn't the right thing. As a lawyer, you know that more than most. How many cases of domestic abuse have you handled?"

"That has nothing to do with Grant."

"Of course not. I'm just saying that staying together isn't always the right thing." She winked at him, trying to lighten the moment. "And some of us were smart enough to stay single and happy."

He pursed his lips and studied her for a long moment. "I think we oughta fix that. Find you the right fellow and get you married off."

"The right fellow was never avail—" She broke off, appalled at what she'd almost said.

The teasing glint in Warren's eye disappeared. "I'm sorry, Gracey. I always figured him for a fool."

Grace's mouth fell open. She snapped it shut and floundered for something to say. Had it been that obvious? Had the entire high school class known? Had *he?*

It shouldn't matter, after over forty years. But she still thought of him…and knew she would until the day she died.

JILL SHADED HER eyes as she stepped out of the hospital after her rounds on Sunday afternoon. Blinding sunlight reflected off the new snow that blanketed the first shift's cars in the employee parking lot.

She'd arrived just an hour ago, and her car stood out like a black sheep in a flock of white—except there was someone out there, leaning against the hood.

With a *bear?*

She blinked, squinting into the sunshine, then resolutely started for the far end of the lot. Someone waiting for his wife, probably, or fiancée. The receptionist's boyfriend came for her most every day, but he usually parked his little Mustang in front.

Curious, now, she stepped up her pace, welcoming the crisp bite of cold air and the crunch of snow beneath her leather boots. Halfway across the lot she finally recognized Grant's navy ski jacket and the red hat he wore on the coldest days.

He was waiting out here in the cold to talk? In ten-below weather? She trudged on, sorting through his possible reasons. Perhaps he'd taken care of some detail for their divorce—finally untangled the complexities of the contract they'd signed for the house, the old liens against it or the aberration in the property line that dated back seventy-three years.

As she drew closer, he flashed a brief smile, his teeth white against the darker tone of his face. She'd always deemed it an injustice that he tanned so easily—even on bright winter days.

"Hello," he called out. "Thought I'd try to catch you before you left."

She frowned, suddenly wary at his almost friendly tone, and jingled the keys in her coat pocket. "What's up? Something new about the divorce?"

"Working on it. Now that I'm back here for a while…" He shrugged. "Shouldn't take long."

The dog at his side was huge, furry and obviously devoted, given the way it stared at Grant's face. Back when they'd been living in Chicago, he'd sworn he'd *never* get a dog.

"You got a *dog?*"

The fine lines at the corners of his eyes deepened. "Actually, I'm serving as transport. Her name's Sadie."

Jill wished she'd chosen something warmer than her dressy leather boots and a cropped woolen jacket. She stamped her feet to regain circulation. "And your point is?"

"She's a present."

She had a troubling premonition as she took in the sheer overwhelming volume of dog sitting next to him. It had to weigh a ton. Maybe two. "So you're on your way to deliver her, right? Say, to an old friend?"

"Yep."

Relieved, she skirted her front bumper and started tapping in the car's key code. "Don't let me hold you up, then."

Grant followed her and braced a hand on the roof of her car. The dog sat between them and looked back and forth between their faces, clearly perplexed.

"You need to hear about this old girl. A sad tale. Abandoned by her parents, cast out into the world. Thought she'd found true love, only to be abandoned once again because she was…" he thought for a moment "…misunderstood by someone who wasn't worthy of her, anyway. Then she went on to great heroism—only to find herself homeless again."

"Only a lawyer could come up with a spiel like that," Jill said dryly. Despite all the bitterness between them, Grant could still be a charming man when he made the effort. "Who had her?"

"Phil."

"Okay, definitely not worthy. Whose life did she save?"

"Mine."

"Really."

"Just yesterday. Crazy client. Big. Mean. Guns. Tattoos everywhere, a motorcycle gang at his back, ready to charge."

"So what she really did was…?"

"Scared a deadbeat dad. Made him fall over."

"I bet he deserved it." Jill laughed, unable to help herself even though she had a strong suspicion about the next answer. "And you're giving her to…?"

"You."

So he'd charmed her for a purpose—just as she'd guessed. Jill finished the last two numbers of the code and opened her door. "Nope. As you can see, I don't have room."

"I deliver."

"No." She slid behind the wheel and fitted her key into the ignition. "No, no and no."

"Think of the benefits."

"If I start spinning wool, I'll give you a call." But still, she couldn't help but reach out to stroke the dog's black coat. Thick and soft, it sparkled in the sunlight. And her eyes…huge, liquid brown eyes. Gentle. *Pleading.* "You know I love dogs, but I have a career. I'm gone all day and sometimes at night. All night even, if I'm on call."

"You're alone in a big house. On a lonely, isolated, dead-end road."

"I've got a security system, a phone and Badger."

"Dogs bark at strangers. They're good protection. You used to tell me," he added softly, "that you thought that house was haunted."

Sometimes she still wondered. But of course, it was just her overactive imagination, coupled with long hours, lack of sleep and living alone. Nothing more than that.

"Look, I'm thinking about the dog. What kind of life would she have with me? She looks like she loves people. You keep her. As I remember, you don't have to worry about being on call at night."

"Can't. You know Dad has kept everything of Mom's just where it was. All those figurines and vases…"

"She looks like an outside dog."

"I thought so, too, but she didn't agree. And at my condo in Kendrick, no pets larger than goldfish are allowed. Period."

"You…have a condo?" The finality of it hit her broadside, not that she cared. She really, *really* didn't care. "You *bought* one?"

"Last month. Though if I'd had a crystal ball, I might have waited."

"Your dad should be done with his rehab in a week, and he's getting stronger every day." Comfortable now that she was on safer ground, the tension in her shoulders eased. "He tells me he's going to travel for a while, but you know he'll be back soon. You won't need to stay in town long."

"Maybe. About the dog—"

"She needs a family, with kids and a fenced yard, Grant."

"She needs a home. Period. Or Phil will send her to a shelter." Grant shook his head. "Where—if she's really lucky—she'll find the right people before her sentence is up."

"You're not playing fair, Grant," Jill shot back. With a breezy wave, she started the car, pulled her door shut and rolled down the window. "Advertise her. Ask around. I'll bet you find just the right people if you only try."

All the way out of town she tapped her fingers on the steering wheel, feeling relief, tinged with regret, at her escape.

She'd made the right decision, she decided as she

headed up Bitter Hollow Road. Badger was more company than anyone needed.

Grant certainly hadn't tried to give her the dog out of any sense of affection. They'd barely been on speaking terms the past few months. He just hadn't wanted to be bothered with the animal's care.

And how could she possibly manage a buffalo like Sadie?

CHAPTER SIX

GRACE PULLED TO a stop in front of the high school on Monday morning, put the car in park and pocketed the keys. "I'm not sure what Principal Travers wants, Ross. Maybe something more about your transfer here, or about how long you plan to stay."

Ross slouched deeper in the seat next to her, the tips of his ears red as he watched the flood of students walk into the building. Embarrassed, probably, by the fact that she was not only there, but was planning to walk in with him like some mom with a third-grader, in full view of the classroom windows.

"Look, why don't you go on in. I'll follow in a couple minutes." She dug in her purse and found her cell phone. "I...have to make a quick call to the hospital, since I'll be a little late this morning."

He opened the door and slid out like melted butter, all long legs and fluid grace, and sauntered into the school without looking back.

Except for the deep purple bruise on his cheek and

the Ace wrap on his wrist, he showed no outward signs of his accident on Friday. At home he still favored his right leg, though, when he thought she wasn't looking, and she'd seen him pop a couple of Tylenol before they left the house this morning.

Boys, she mused. Being macho was tough on all of them at times, but Ross's intermittent belligerence and bravado went deeper. The phone call from his mother last week had made him retreat even further.

When Grace arrived in the waiting area of the principal's office a couple minutes later, Ross had already slumped in a chair set off by itself on the other side of the secretary's desk.

The secretary was new, but the area was unchanged. Grace smiled to herself as a hundred memories flooded back, of all the times she'd been in this office with a newly arrived youngster, or had come to advocate for one of her special-needs kids who'd caused a ruckus of one type or another.

There'd been the tough ones, too, inner-city bred and ready to take on the world. But they'd all turned out well. Those were the good old days, filled with joy and frustration, worries and the deepest sense of pride.

And now, she had this one last chance to do it all again.

"Mr. Travers will see you now," said the pert young thing behind the receptionist's desk. "Down the hall behind me, second door on your left."

"Believe me, I remember." She walked to his office and took the same old chair across from Dan Travers's desk, where even more memories assailed her as she studied the family photos he'd hung on the wall. His children. Grandchildren.

Many of his late wife, Leah, a woman Grace had once envied for her place in Dan's life, but in the end could only admire for her gracious spirit. Leah had become a close friend, and her early death left an empty place in Grace's life.

Ross ambled into the room, scanned the layout and dropped into the chair next to Grace without saying a word.

Dan walked in a moment later. Tall and lean, with a full head of silver hair, he'd changed very little with age.

"Sorry to keep you two waiting," he said, reaching across his desk to shake Grace's hand. "Brings back old times, doesn't it?"

"It does indeed," she murmured. His hand was warm and hard and, heaven help her, it still made her heart falter after all these years. "I'm so happy to have my great-nephew with me now. Makes me feel young again."

Dan leaned back in his chair and studied Ross over the edge of his wire rims. "We're glad to have him here. It's been what—a week, now? Excepting last Friday, of course. How are you feeling, son?"

Ross hitched a shoulder.

"He was lucky," Grace offered in the ensuing silence. "A split-second difference, and it could have been tragic." She reached over to pat Ross's knee. "I've given thanks every day since."

"Ross?" Dan prompted.

The boy fidgeted in his chair, his eyes downcast. "I'm okay."

Dan frowned. "That's what I really wanted to talk about today, Ross. I'm concerned about you."

"Concerned? About what?" Grace glanced from Ross to Dan. "Has there been any trouble?"

"Ross is often late for school, and his fifth- and sixth-hour teachers tell me he's been skipping out early." Dan braced his elbows on the armrests of his chair and steepled his fingers. "I've had some other teachers tell me he isn't completing his homework and is apathetic in class. A few times, he's been sarcastic. Is that true, Ross?"

"Dunno," he mumbled, sullen. "Maybe."

Just one child under her roof, and for only a week so far, and she was already failing him? "Ross, if that's the case, we're going to—"

Dan held up his hand, then shifted his attention back to Ross. "We need to get to the bottom of this. Your scores on the annual, nationwide tests last year hit the ninety-fifth percentile across the board, so most of the general studies here should be child's play. You could ace every one of them."

Ross hitched a foot across the opposite thigh and picked at the frayed edge of his jeans. "Maybe."

"You're just a sophomore now, but with the right motivation you could be in line for big scholarships. Yet I've looked over your old records, and if you continue the way you're going, you'll have a hard time graduating."

He didn't look up.

Dan casually played with a pencil on his desk, rotating it between his fingers, but his gaze was fixed on the boy. "I just want to make sure you get off to the best possible start here, and I think you're capable of accomplishing a great deal. What do you think?"

When Ross didn't answer, the principal smiled. "We may have tougher behavior guidelines here, so you should be aware of that. We have very low tolerance for absenteeism, and we insist on respect. That said, I hope you have a positive experience here, and wonder if you might be a little bored in our regular classes. If you're here next fall, we'll definitely look into advanced placement." Dan pursed his lips. "Being new to a school is a huge stressor for any student—especially midyear. I'd say that's a given. Change is difficult, even for adults. And it can be hard to find your way at first. But I don't think that nails it either. Not completely."

Ross fidgeted uneasily.

"I know it's tough, moving so far from home. A

guy can get down when he misses his home and family."

Horrified, Ross lifted his gaze to Dan for a moment. "You think I'm some kind of *mental* case?"

"No, of course not. I think you're a bright—even gifted—student. But a couple of your teachers are a little concerned, and they've come to me. I want you to know that my door is always open, if you want to talk to someone."

The boy's cheeks flamed red. He shot to his feet and paced the room, then spun back to face Dan and Grace. "I get jerked out of my old school, away from my friends, and dumped in this stupid town. My mom runs off and marries a creep the minute I'm gone. I should be *happy?* I hate it here. And now I can't even go home again. Not with Tony—"

He broke off, his jaw set and his hands clenched at his side. He was fairly vibrating with anger. Dan and Grace exchanged glances, and Grace knew what he was thinking.

Apparently Ross did too, because he swore under his breath. "*No* guy is gonna knock me around and keep his front teeth."

"I don't doubt that for a minute." Dan studied the pencil in his hand for a few moments, until the tension in the room seemed to ease. "What I propose is this. I know you aren't happy. No one would be, in your situation, but sometimes it helps to find a good listener. If you don't feel comfortable talking to me, we have an excellent counselor here." Ross bristled, and Dan added quietly, "Just think about it. What do you have to lose?"

A bell rang, and Ross looked at the clock. "Can I go now?"

Dan stood and offered his hand until Ross reluctantly accepted it. "Get a pass from my secretary as you leave. We'll meet again next week." He glanced at the planner on the desk. "Is ten o'clock, same day all right?"

Grace nodded and started to rise, but Dan shook his head. "Wait."

After Ross was gone, he leaned forward, his hands clasped on his desk. "I've requested additional records from his old schools, because one teacher is questioning the possibility of mild learning disabilities. She says he seems frustrated by some of the reading assignments."

"I thought you said he was smart!"

"Many of the LD kids are gifted. *Highly* intelligent. Maybe he just needs a little extra help from our resource teacher, who works with these kids all the time. Ross probably won't want to hear it, though. Guys his age think we're talking about a weakness that will set them apart."

"He hasn't had a stable life," Grace murmured.

"And we want to help him all we can. Maybe he's

fine. Maybe the fact that he's acting out and having other problems is just a temporary reaction to all of the changes in his life. But if he's starting to spiral downward, it isn't something to ignore."

ROSS SHOULDERED HIS heavy backpack and joined the throng of students passing between classes, his head down. It was easier this way, staying anonymous. Avoiding the curious stares of the students who'd been here all year—and had probably lived here all their lives.

They didn't need an outsider butting in. He'd learned that during all of his moves in the Chicago area, when his mom was still switching from job to job, from one boyfriend to another.

But now he caught curious glances as some of the students passed him. At the bruises on his face and the bandage on his wrist. The first rule of being the new kid in school was to simply blend in and not be weird, but today he might as well have been wearing a neon sign.

An older kid—the hulking, football type—stopped him. "Hey, what happened? Get in a fight?"

A clone of the first guy came up on his other side and jostled him. "Yeah, what's up, dude?"

The undercurrent of challenge in his tone was unmistakable. And though Ross was just as tall, they each outweighed him by a good fifty to seventy-five pounds. If they got rough, he'd be hamburger. He kept walking, his eyes fixed on the classroom door at the end of the hallway. "Just an accident."

"Oh, right. You walked into a door?" The first one hooted. He gave Ross a shove against the other guy. "Like I believe that."

The two guys slammed to a halt, and with his attention on them, he barely had time to avoid hitting the girl who'd planted herself right in front of him.

His gaze swept past her Doc Martens, designer jeans and red sweater to her stormy expression. Mandy Welbourne.

She jabbed a forefinger into one of the jocks' chests. "*Boyd*, lay off."

The guy probably went by a nickname like Rock or Terminator, and he blushed red at the use of his given name.

"You too, *Teddy*." She gave them each a look of pure disgust. "You guys were nice, in second grade."

Uneasy, aware of the silence in the hallway, Ross tried to back away but was trapped by the growing crowd.

"You wonder what happened to this guy? I lost control of my car, and had an accident. I hit him, but he…" she flicked a glance at Ross, warning him to be quiet "…he still rushed over to help me. If he hadn't been there, I don't know what I would have done."

If she wasn't in the drama club, she was wasting a lot of talent. The crowd murmured, casting appraising glances at Ross and curious ones at the jocks, probably wondering what they'd done to incur Mandy's wrath.

The bell rang, and the students dispersed like a startled school of minnows, leaving Mandy and Ross alone in the hall.

"I'm so sorry," she said. "For the accident, and for—this. Kids can be stupid, you know? Ted and Boyd are two of the worst."

He felt himself blush. "I was stupid to be out on my bike in the winter."

"Friends?" Her soft blue eyes twinkled as she offered her hand.

He shook hands awkwardly. "Well, uh, guess we better go."

"Guess so." She hitched the strap of her backpack higher on her shoulder. "See you around?"

He nodded, suddenly tongue-tied, and watched her walk into a room two doors down.

She was pretty. She was obviously popular, fearless and had a strong sense of justice. But she probably defended any loser in trouble, so there was no point in even thinking about her.

Mandy Welbourne was way out of his league.

AFTER A HECTIC day at the clinic followed by two hours at the hospital, Jill longed for the peace and quiet of home—such as it was, with Badger on the prowl—and a long, hot bath.

She wasn't prepared for the sight of hundreds of knee-high red flags circling her house, fluttering in the breeze, or Sadie sitting on her porch.

Or the fact that the lights were blazing.

She sat in her car with the motor still running, her wrists draped over the steering wheel. Exactly what part of her refusal had Grant misunderstood? She'd been very clear, and he'd ignored her.

Which was, she reflected, a rather succinct summary of their entire relationship.

Muttering to herself, she put the car in the garage and strode up the sidewalk. Sadie thumped her tail eagerly on the porch, her eyes bright and curious.

"I suppose you think you're staying," she said as she crossed the porch and unlocked the door. "But this is a visit. A *brief* one. Now, where's your friend?"

The dog shivered—probably from anticipation rather than the cold, given its massive coat—and she whistled it into the house.

Sure enough, Grant had brought roaster-sized dog dishes for water and food, which were sitting by the back door. A fifty-pound bag of dog food leaned against the closet.

Sadie bounded through the main floor of the house, then returned to the kitchen and rested her nose on the counter to stare at the cookie jar.

Jill hung up her jacket, then nudged the filled dog food dish with the toe of her shoe. "This is yours. Not the cookies."

At a light knock on the door she turned and saw Grant through the glass. When he let himself in, she met him with folded arms. "Do you see anything different in here?"

He glanced around. "Just Sadie, and maybe those flowers on the table…"

"Stop. Why on earth did you bring her here?"

"Maybe we can consider her a loan?"

"You can't loan out a dog. They get *attached* to people. It's not fair."

"If you fight me for her, I'll let you win." He smiled, apparently thinking his old charm would work again. *As if.*

But then Sadie's big brown eyes veered from the cookie jar to Jill, and her resolve faltered. "I suppose those little flags stuck in the snow mark the perimeter of an electronic fence?"

"Right, just until she learns where her boundaries are. The system is entirely portable." He tipped his head toward a small, gray radio-transmitter box plugged into an outlet by the door. "If you check her collar, you'll see a little radio device. If she tries to go too far, she'll feel a tingle."

Dubious, Jill frowned at the tiny plastic gadget on Sadie's collar. "And that's going to stop her?"

"She used the same system at Phil's and is already trained to respect it."

Sadie sidled over and leaned her broad head against Jill's thigh. Warm, trusting.

"She'll be good for you," he continued. "No prowler will dare come within ten feet of this house, I guarantee it."

"You brought her here for your convenience, not mine. I still can't believe you did this without my permission. I said *no*."

"I was banking on Sadie's charm. Phil was serious about getting rid of her, and you've got this big place…"

"…which is still half yours. Except I'm the one who'll have to care for her, and I'm rarely home."

"Please?"

Jill sighed, dropping a hand to the dog's silky head to rub her behind one ear. "Just until you find a better place."

"Understood."

"Do you? This is what happened in our marriage, Grant. We never really listened to each other."

"You're right, of course. On all counts." His smile faded. "I thought you loved dogs, but bringing Sadie here was presumptuous. I'll take her back."

"No, she can stay while you're living at your dad's place, but she should have a big family. Kids to play with." Jill glanced at the clock above the stove. "Not a place where she's always alone and bored until late in the day."

"Understood." Grant hesitated, one hand on the door. "I'll…be on my way, then. If you need anything, just call."

"Thanks." But she wouldn't call, and knew he didn't expect it, either. They were a poor match and neither of them had changed.

It was better to leave well enough alone.

CHAPTER SEVEN

"I'M LEAVING FOR Florida when I get out of here,"
Warren announced.

"What?" Grant stared at his elderly father. "Even
after another week of rehab—which both Jill and the
cardiologist recommend, by the way—you'll be too
weak. Isn't this pushing things just a little?"

"Nope." Warren paced the room and then dropped
into one of the high-backed visitor chairs in his room.
"After almost two weeks at Blackberry Hill Memorial
I'm so stir-crazy I could fly on my own power." He
turned, brandishing several pieces of paper that had
been lying on the bed. "Today, I learned how to get
e-tickets on the Internet, and I researched flights."

Bemused, Grant took the papers and skimmed
over the flight dates and times. "How on earth did
you manage this in the hospital?"

"You young folks aren't the only ones who understand the Internet. Doc Olson was on call one night,
and he let me use the computer in the doctor's lounge."

"Your old golf buddy?"

"One and the same." With a smug smile, Warren took the papers from Grant. "I told him it was either that computer, or I was going AWOL to the town library in my hospital pj's."

Grant laughed. "I think that's AMA, Dad— against medical advice."

"Whatever." Warren tapped the paper into a neat stack and slid it into the drawer of the tray table by his bed.

"I'm not sure this is a great idea, you gallivanting all over when you've been so ill."

"Son, if I keel over on a Florida golf course in February, you'll know I died happy." He impatiently crossed one leg over the other, drumming his fingers on the arm of the chair. "You're sure you don't mind staying at my house and running the office till I get back?"

"Whether I'm here or at the Kendrick office, I'm still part of the same practice."

His father gave him a long, assessing look. "Not exactly what you'd planned on, though. You were on the fast track to a big partnership. Fancy house. You can say no to all of this here, and be on your way."

"I had six years at the firm in Chicago, and that was more than enough. When you had your first heart attack I was more than ready to leave."

"No regrets?"

"None."

"And this town? Not some other place?"

"Where else? I've got family here, and northern Wisconsin is like paradise compared to Chicago."

"When I'm gone, Phil will have the Kendrick office and you'll have this one—if you want it."

"Something I don't even want to think about, Dad. You should live to be a hundred."

"Who knows," Warren said with a noncommittal smile. "I might even come back from Florida and decide I want to retire, and then you'll need to take over even sooner." He waggled one bushy eyebrow, à la Groucho Marx. "While I'm away, you could take care of a few other things…like that divorce of yours. Do you even know what day it is?"

"The fourteenth."

"Valentine's Day. And what are you doing? Sitting with an old man in a hospital."

"Dad—"

"Biggest mistake you ever made, in my book. It isn't too late, unless you let someone else nab her."

But the finality in Jill's farewell last night had echoed his own feelings. There was no going back.

JILL KNOCKED ON the door of the tiny rental house, waited for a moment, then pushed it open a few inches. "Patsy, is it okay if I come in?"

The shades were drawn, the darkened living room

illuminated only by a small lamp in the corner. The hospital bed set up in the middle of the room was a jumble of bedding that had been pushed aside.

Toys cluttered the floor.

"Hi," Patsy murmured. She shifted in the bed and smiled. "Sorry I'm not ready for company."

Jill approached, glad to see that her patient's hair was clean and her nightgown fresh. She'd finally accepted oxygen, and seemed more comfortable now that she didn't need to struggle so much to breathe. "I know Alison and Ben must be in school, but where is everyone else?"

"My sister took Zoe with her to the grocery store. They'll be back soon."

Jill bent to check the setting on the oxygen tank. "How are you doing with hospice? Everything going all right?"

"Oh, yes." She took a few deeper breaths from the oxygen cannulas positioned beneath her nose. "I'm so happy to be home with my kids."

"They must be very glad you're here." A nurse came every night now, and Patsy's sister Barb stayed through the day. "Have you used the video camera yet?"

Patsy nodded. "Barb runs it for me. I've filled three cassettes already." Winded, she paused and took another deep breath.

Jill checked her pulse, then took a stethoscope from her bag and listened to her lung sounds. "I know hospice is on top of things, but I like checking in on you, too. Are they keeping you comfortable enough with your morphine?"

"As much…as I want."

"Last time I came, I told Barb to be sure to give me the tapes when you're done. I'll copy them onto DVDs. One for each child, and some extras."

"Thanks…that means a lot to me." Her eyes fluttered shut for a moment. "Got…so much left to do."

She drifted off to sleep, her face a mask of weariness. Jill sat by her bed until Barb returned with Zoe.

The older woman smiled when she came in the door with the child in her arms. "I saw your car out front," she whispered. "Thank you for coming."

"I just wish there was more I could do for her." From the first, something about the young woman had struck a chord in Jill. Professional distance hadn't been possible in this case.

"Could you step outside with me for a minute?" Barb asked. "I won't keep you long."

Jill followed her into the small fenced-in backyard, where she let Zoe run to the snow-covered sandbox.

"You probably know about Kurt," Barb said in a low voice. "Do you ever see newspapers from Green Bay?"

"I've heard rumors."

Barb shook her head. "Patsy doesn't know, but I'm going to have to tell her soon. She always figured he'd automatically get custody of the kids, whether she liked it or not. But now…"

"I hear he's in a great deal of trouble. Finagling prescriptions for himself was bad enough. Letting his buddy overdose and leaving him to die was horrific."

"My husband thinks he'll serve federal time for multiple drug charges and manslaughter."

"I hope he's right." Jill watched Zoe scooping snow into a bucket. "What will happen with the kids? Do you think Kurt's new wife will take them?"

"Not on your life." Barb snorted in disgust. "I always figured her for a gold digger. Sure enough, she filed for divorce within a week of his arrest."

"Who does that leave, then? You, surely."

"We're barely making it as it is, because my husband's disabled. But I would sure try. I love those kids like my own."

"They'll qualify for social security benefits, probably, and other forms of aid. But what about Kurt's side of the family?"

"His parents are old and he's an only child. It scares me to think the kids might end up in foster care if Kurt goes to prison. Could that happen?"

Jill bit her lower lip. "I can't answer that."

"I don't know if it's possible to arrange a private adoption fast enough…or how much time Patsy has left for making her decisions. It's going to break her heart if she can't be sure her kids are safe before she dies."

"My…husband does pro bono work on the side. I can ask him to help, if you'd like."

Barb grabbed Jill's hand. "Oh, would you? Please?"

"I'll stop by his office on my way back to the clinic. If he can't take care of this, he'll know who to ask."

NATALIE ZIMMERMAN RAISED both hands to her temples and ran her fingers through her long, auburn hair, then settled back in her chair and crossed her legs.

The action, Grant noticed, showcased her tight sweater and substantial…attributes.

Once upon a time, when he'd been single—no, wait. He practically *was* single. But nothing she offered appealed to him now. Not after Jill, though that relationship was over.

Especially because of that.

"I'm glad you could see me today," she murmured. "You were such a help to me last fall. With…Ray."

Grant nodded. Her husband had been difficult, all right. A restraining order and two arrests for violating it didn't seem to faze him—until an outstanding warrant from Florida caught up with him.

"I've never been happier than the day he was sent down there to serve time." Her laughter was throaty, provocative. "I was such a fool, getting hooked up with a loser like him."

"From all accounts, you weren't the first." And when the guy got out, she wouldn't be the last. Ray had a five-page rap sheet for everything from assault to burglary—and attempted-murder charges, which were only dropped after the sole witness failed to show up in court. He'd been married at least three times…and two of those wives had disappeared. Natalie was the lucky one.

It was hard to reconcile the confident person sitting across from him with the frightened young woman who'd called him at all hours of the day and night last fall. "You look as if you've been doing well."

"I have a little salon over in Greenburg, now." She tossed her hair. "Finally, I get to use my education." She leaned forward, offering an ample view down her low-cut sweater. "If you hadn't been able to meet me when Ray was off doing construction…"

The irony was that nothing was ever truly secret in a small town, and, while he'd managed to successfully handle the end of her volatile marriage, the subsequent rumors had helped end his own.

"I'm glad it worked out for you." He gathered a pile of manila folders and tapped them into a neat stack on his desk. "What can I help you with now?"

"I'm looking into some investment property in Greenburg. I don't have much money, but there's a nice corner lot on Main. I need some advice…." With animated gestures, she spent the next fifteen minutes describing her plans to develop a gift shop in the space, along with a new location for her salon.

"And you know, I'd be interested in bringing in some additional investors. The building next door is available, too—just think what all of this could do for that town."

The front door chimed, and someone stepped inside. After a moment, Grant heard footsteps coming down the hall.

He glanced at the open appointment book on his desk. "Excuse me for a minute, would you?"

She touched his arm as he passed. "I'm sorry—time flies when I talk to you. Maybe we can meet another time? Soon?"

He'd just made it to the doorway when Jill appeared.

"Hi, I…" Her smile faded when she looked over his shoulder. "I'm sorry. I should have called first."

"Wait. Can you come back a little later? Say, an hour?"

Her eyes flashed fire for just an instant. "I need to talk to you about a child custody situation, but I'll just call. Really—I didn't mean to interrupt."

With a cool smile, she turned on her heel and left.

NATALIE STAYED ANOTHER forty-five minutes, radiating signals that she was available. Grant kept a careful distance. When she left, he'd tried to make it more than clear that he wasn't interested. Knowing Natalie, the message probably hadn't gotten through.

After that, Leo Crupper kept his appointment to

discuss a new living will, and a young father came in to talk about trust accounts for his two daughters. All in all, a productive day, though now and then Grant's attention had strayed to the clock.

When the last client left at a quarter past five, Grant saw that the evening sky had already darkened to pewter.

Jill was probably finishing up her afternoon appointments. And he…

He had another hour of paperwork before he could even think about leaving. Or, he could stuff it in his briefcase and take it home, and maybe swing by her clinic on his way.

That was definitely the better option, for Sadie's sake.

Jill had agreed to take her, but he'd hardly been fair, dropping the dog off like that. Given the dog's size and obsession over slippers, throw rugs and underwear, she might have done a lot of damage already.

And if Jill got upset and decided not to keep her, the dog didn't have many options left. The local vet hadn't known of anyone looking for a very large dog. The billboard at the grocery was festooned with dozens of flyers for free puppies and kittens.

And it was hardly likely that Sadie had reformed in response to Grant's Good Behavior lecture on the trip to Chapel Hill.

Maybe he'd need to stop by, now and then, to

check on her. Offer to dog-sit during the day now and then, so she wouldn't be alone for so many hours and looking for something to chew. Maybe…

Maybe he was just looking for an excuse.

Grant locked the front door of the office, and checked all the windows on his way down the hall. The phone rang before he reached the back door. A quick glance at the caller ID read Unknown, so he left it for the answering machine.

Ten minutes later, he'd parked at the back of the clinic, where Jill's office nurse, Donna Iverson, was just stepping out the door with her purse slung over her shoulder.

She spared him a dismissive glance, then pointedly ignored him as she swept past his car.

"Hey, Donna," he called after her. "Is Jill still here?"

Her thin smile was as cold as the frosty air. "She won't be done for a good long while. Maybe an hour."

"Thanks." Remembering the woman's fierce support of Jill last fall when their marriage had floundered, Grant mentally divided that time by the Donna Factor, and figured Jill was probably nearly done. "I'll wait."

Donna sniffed and moved on to her own vehicle. And sure enough, Jill appeared at the back door of the clinic moments after Donna drove away.

Grant got out of his car to meet her. "Sorry I couldn't talk to you earlier."

She waved away his apology. "Understandable. I'm sure you were…busy."

"With a client, Jill." He counted to ten. "Long day?"

"You might say that." She glanced over his shoulder toward his truck, and her eyes narrowed. "Is this another animal delivery, or is one beast enough for this week?"

"I've been meaning to talk to you about that."

"No. More. Dogs."

He held out his hands in surrender. "None. In fact, I stopped to make sure you're getting along with the one you have."

"Really." Jill folded her arms across her chest. "Nice of you to take that into consideration now, Grant. Did you know about Sadie's penchant for lace? Silk? Slippers? Surely Phil told you some of this before you hauled her away."

Grant winced. "A lot of damage?"

"She drags my lingerie all over the house, and thinks slippers are prey. She and Badger have *not* come to terms over the territory, and the yowling and barking is enough to raise the dead."

"I thought she'd be good company. Good protection. But if you truly don't want her…"

"I didn't say that. She's more of a pussycat than Badger is. But I still think it was manipulative of you to just drop her off."

"That's why I'm here. Maybe I should take her

with me to work, now and then, so she won't be alone so much. How is it going so far—other than the clothing and the cat?"

"Actually…" Jill looked away. "You'll probably think this is weird, because I know you've never had the same feelings in the house that I have…"

That was the understatement of the year.

Jill had fallen in love with that Victorian monstrosity at first sight. He'd seen the facts—a future filled with astronomical restoration costs and crushing bills for heating and air.

From the moment they'd signed the mortgage, the place had been the source of one argument after another until they were barely on speaking terms. The odd thing was that until they'd moved in, he'd never had such a short fuse. Neither had she.

"I know what you're thinking," she retorted. "But this isn't about the house. It's Sadie. When I came home from work yesterday, I thought she'd be anxious to get outside after being in all day. But she didn't meet me at the door, and didn't come when I called."

Bad news. "She had accidents in the house?"

"None. I found her in the parlor, by that old rocker you brought down from the attic last summer. She was just sitting by it, wagging her tail." Shivering, Jill fastened the top button of her coat. "And I'd swear, that chair was rocking."

CHAPTER EIGHT

"IF THAT PLACE spooks you, you shouldn't stay," Grant said slowly. "You could move someplace else. It's a money pit, anyway."

"I know you didn't want to buy it in the first place, but Chapel Hill is a dream come true for me," she said firmly. "Maybe it has a few odd drafts. A feeling of…I don't know, loneliness, maybe. But I still plan to buy you out when we finalize the divorce."

"Do what you want. I really don't care as long as I'm not a part of it any longer."

"Do you remember us back in college, talking about the future?" A wistful smile lit her face. "How I used to sketch the house that I wanted?"

"A Victorian." He sighed, remembering her single-minded determination to buy this particular house. He'd brought plenty of his own faults to the marriage, but she'd certainly put her career and the blasted house far ahead of him.

"I'm sorry about interrupting you at work this afternoon."

"Whatever you might think, that was an *appointment* with Natalie Zimmerman. Nothing personal."

"That doesn't matter." She waved away his explanation as if it were no more than an annoying mosquito. "I was only there to ask a favor for a terminal patient of mine. She has very limited resources, and there'll be custody issues with her children. If you don't have space in your schedule for some pro bono work, could you make a referral?"

Despite her veneer of professionalism, there was definitely a note of underlying worry in Jill's voice. "Of course. Tell her she can stop in anytime."

"It's too late for that, really." Jill bent over her purse, retrieved a pen and notepad and scrawled a name and address. "Go see her as soon as you can. She's under hospice care in her home. Her sister Barb is there all day, in case you need a witness for a will."

He tucked the paper into his inside jacket pocket. "Tomorrow afternoon."

"Thanks." She hesitated, then offered her hand. "She's so worried."

"No problem." But Jill's handshake was. Just last fall it would have been a kiss. Yet her casual touch still brought back memories that had no place in the carefully polite relationship they had now. He held her hand for a second and released it. "Is this someone you're close to?"

"Patsy and her kids have been patients for a year.

Her kids are all adorable and so very young. It's been impossible to keep any professional distance, knowing what they're all facing."

He took a step back, needing more than just *physical* distance, and glanced at his watch. "I'd better run. Should I take Sadie to my office tomorrow?"

"If you really want to, but I think she'll be okay." Jill wrapped her wool scarf more snugly around her neck. "I'm…glad we can still be civil, despite everything."

Her voice trailed off, and he wondered if she ever felt the same weight of sadness and loss that he did. Probably not. She'd always been too upfront, cool and businesslike to waste time on things that couldn't be changed.

"I'm thankful, too," he said. "Take care."

He watched her get into her car and drive away, then got behind the wheel of his truck. She turned right down Main toward the hospital for her late-afternoon rounds. He turned left and started for home.

On a whim, he pulled to a stop in front of Bailey's grocery and strolled inside to get a box of dog biscuits.

The young guy at the cash register—early twenties, maybe—gave Grant a hard look as he counted back the change.

His name badge said Alexander Walthan and, sure enough, the tip of a snake tattoo showed just below the edge of his shirt cuff. This kid was one of several grandchildren Hal Walthan had recently disowned.

"You're my grandfather's lawyer." Alexander's lip curled.

"Am I?" Grant folded the bills into his wallet.

"My mom pointed you out on the street. Hal's like, totally senile," the kid snarled. "Mom says you're helping him make crazy decisions that won't ever stand up in court. She's gonna put him in a home."

"Really." The kid had the bloodshot eyes and dilated pupils of someone who'd had more than soda and Twinkies over his lunch break. Grant lifted his grocery bag and turned to go. "See you around."

Hal had seemed perfectly competent, and meeting the kid had just confirmed it. If the family tried to contest his will, there'd be no way in hell they'd have a chance of winning.

Grant planned to stand behind it one hundred percent.

ROSS SHOULDERED HIS backpack and trailed after the kids leaving the seventh-hour language arts class.

Since the appointment with the principal and Grace on Monday, he'd made it to all his classes. He hadn't cut out early. He'd tried—with some success—to keep his mouth shut during each class. It didn't make being here any easier, but at least the teachers didn't hassle him as much.

Word had spread like wildfire through the school about Mandy hitting him with her car, and her sharp defense of him in the hall…and also about his little visit to the principal's office that morning.

He'd been just an oddity before—a kid from Chicago with different clothes and no friends. Now, he heard whispers behind his back and felt the stares as he walked down the hall. *What a jerk. Who does he think he is? I hear he's a dealer, and got sent up here…*

The cliques were so tight in this small town that he'd given up trying to be friendly after his first day. They could think whatever they damn well pleased. When summer came he was heading south. Maybe not back to Mom's, but somewhere. *Anywhere* but here.

Something soft brushed against his arm and he pulled sharply away, trying to maintain his isolation in the crowd of students heading for home.

"Hey, stranger," said a feminine voice, and again, he felt a soft touch on his arm.

He looked down to find Mandy Welbourne matching his stride and grinning up at him, her pale blond ponytail swinging and her lips shiny with pink lipstick. "Hey."

She rolled her eyes. "I'm *still* not supposed to talk to you because of the insurance thing, but I think that's stupid, don't you? It's just *sooo* out there to think that there's gonna be a big lawsuit, or something. But my dad is just weird, you know?"

Ross kept walking, at a complete loss over what to say to that.

"We've got two classes together," she continued blithely, as if they were actually having a conversation. "Third-hour algebra and sixth-hour computer skills. You're always way in the back during computer, though." She laughed. "I stay up in the front, because I need lots of help."

He shrugged.

"Kids say you're really stuck-up, and that you've been in big trouble down in Chicago." A tiny frown line formed between her eyebrows. "Personally, I think you're just shy."

Ross felt himself redden. Being considered a troublemaker meant the other guys gave him space. Being shy just sounded *weak*. He cleared his throat and dropped his voice an octave. "I'm not."

"So, what do you do for fun? I mean, like, what cool stuff did you do in the city?"

They'd reached the front entry of the building, where icy wind blasted down the hall as the student in front of them opened the door. Ross zipped his jacket and pulled on his gloves. He wondered what a rich girl did with *her* time. Ski trips, maybe. Trips to Florida and Cancun for winter break. "Just hung out, I guess."

"Want a ride home? It's got to be thirty below out there, and you've got a long walk home."

After meeting her dad, he knew *that* wasn't a real good idea. "No, thanks."

She looped her arm in his as they stepped outside, and pressed against his side so closely he nearly fell out the door from shock. "I'm for sure giving you a ride. Hey, I creamed your bike and I owe you." She nudged him with her elbow. "I'll probably lose my school driver's permit over that, so you'd better take the ride while you can. If I lose it, I'll have to wait until my birthday in June for my full license."

Despite his protests, she led him out to the parking lot. The wind whistled through the pines rimming the parking lot, kicking up ground blizzards between the rows of cars and making it hard to breathe. By the time they reached her little silver Firebird, his face hurt and his feet were numb.

Luckily, her car started on the second try, and she cranked up the heater. After rubbing her mittened hands together, Mandy shifted the transmission into Reverse and backed out cautiously, then drove slowly out of the lot.

She shot a glance of pure devilment at him. "I'm only supposed to go straight to and from school on my permit, so don't tell. Okay?"

He nodded, though he had a feeling she'd done more than a few things to jeopardize that permit.

All the way to his house, she chattered about school, and her friends, and a school dance coming up in a few weeks. He just listened and nodded, feeling tongue-tied and stupid, until she pulled to a stop to let him out of the car. What did guys talk about with girls? His brain had turned to slush. He opened his door and awkwardly climbed out, hauling his backpack after him. "Uh…thanks. For the ride, I mean."

Her cell phone burst into the *Fraggle Rock* theme song as she leaned across the seat to wave goodbye. "No problem. See you tomorrow?"

"Yeah."

She smiled back, but as he started to close the door, he could hear her talking into her phone. "Yes, Daddy—I know. I'm sorry, I know I shouldn't have, but—*please* Daddy—"

With the door shut tight, he lost the rest of her words. But he looked over his shoulder as he trudged up the front steps of Grace's door, and her car hadn't moved.

Daddy had to be giving her a blistering lecture. Ross waited at the door until she finally drove off, then went inside.

He'd thought his own life sucked…and that hers was charmed. Popularity, looks, brains, money—she seemed to have it all. But maybe it wasn't so easy being a princess after all.

"I DON'T KNOW HOW well this is going," Grace said on a sigh, resigned. "The good thing is that I haven't had any calls from the school all week. The bad thing is that Ross barely talks to me. Ever since his mother's call, he's been simmering."

Erin Reynolds, Blackberry Hill Memorial's administrator, smiled in sympathy. "It can't be easy for him, from what you've said. What will happen if he refuses to go back and live with her?"

"He can stay with me, if he wants to. I'm not sure about any other options. There are some other relatives on his dad's side, but I have no idea how close they are. Certainly none of them are in his old school district."

"Are you two still seeing Dan Travers on Monday?"

"Definitely, though Ross isn't happy about it."

"How about you?" Erin teased. "What's it like, being back in the principal's office again?"

Erin had started working at the hospital last September, and had been entirely too quick to notice Grace's long-standing attraction to her old high-school classmate.

"It's all business. Nothing more than that." Grace knew she was too old to blush and ignored the warmth stealing into her cheeks. Searching for a safer topic, she leaned forward in her chair to turn the silver-framed photograph on Erin's desk. "I'm still hoping you'll bring in an album of photos from your wedding."

Erin and Dr. Reynolds had flown to the Bahamas in January for a beach wedding with her three young children along as attendants. Still tanned from all the sun, she'd positively glowed with happiness ever since their return.

"I will. There are still so many to sort through—digital, as well as 35mm prints. The kids and I thought we should include the entire trip in that album." Erin winked at her. "Maybe you'll be next at the altar."

"Hardly. At my age, I'm just happy to wake up every morning."

"And Dan…?"

"He had Leah. Beautiful, charming, the perfect gracious hostess. What would he want with an old warhorse like me?"

"Oh, Grace. *Really.* You're smart and fun, and you're more active than most people half your age. If he'd just open his eyes, he'd see what a gem you are—and right under his nose, too."

"I've seen some of those younger chicks giving him the eye, Erin. I'm not foolish enough to think I can compete with some forty-year-old, size 10 tootsie."

"Well, he'd be cradle robbing. Men are so ridiculous when they don't go after women their own age." Erin's smile faded. "You aren't still thinking about retiring this summer, are you?"

"I'll be sixty-seven come July."

"And…?"

"I could probably go for another few years, but that's not in the best interest of the hospital."

Grace glanced around the office, feeling suddenly old. She'd been at this hospital under five different administrators—some good, some bad—since she'd started here as a nurse forty-five years ago.

Forty-five years. Where had her life gone? It had been measured as shift duty by a time clock on the wall…and then, by the hectic pace of being director of nursing.

The thought filled her with sadness.

"No one is asking you to retire," Erin said gently. She'd come around the corner of her desk to rest a hand on Grace's shoulder. "It will be nearly impossible to find anyone who can replace you."

"There are plenty of nurses out there."

"None like you." Erin's eyes conveyed her concern. "I know you're under a lot of stress with Ross. If you need some time off, just say the word. You've got months of vacation time saved up, or you could take a leave of absence. Whatever you need."

Grace patted her hand, then lumbered to her feet. "No, I'd better stay. But come summer, you'll have my resignation on your desk."

IF HE NEVER saw Florida again, it would be too soon.

Ray counted out eight hundred dollars in cash and handed it to the eager used-car dealer.

The used-car lot was perfect—a seedy little weed-infested corner in the worst part of town. Not a place that kept good records. The salesman was even better—with his cagey eyes and his wary edge, Ray would've bet a fifty the guy had done time.

The man practically salivated over the pile of fifties in his palm, then smirked as he handed over the keys. He clearly figured he'd received a windfall from a real sucker, getting sticker price for his battered '73 Mustang. He had no idea that the deal—cash, under an assumed name—was Ray's ticket to freedom.

And revenge.

No one got the better of Ray Zimmerman. *No one.*

"You got yourself a real beauty, bud." The guy backed away, nodding, sweat glistening on his ruddy brow.

Ray didn't bother to answer. The car started okay. He'd driven it around the block. Now, it just had to make the sixteen-hundred-mile drive north.

If it hadn't been for his lawyer finagling probation, he'd still be rotting in that lousy dorm with a dozen other inmates.

He threw his duffel bag in the back seat and jerked the vehicle into a sharp three-point turn, then headed north.

There was no hurry. Natalie and her damn lawyer had no idea he was free. And so he would take care, and make no mistakes.

He would plan every move. And in the end, the bitch would be sorry she'd ever dared defy him…and the lawyer would regret the day he was born.

CHAPTER NINE

JILL RUBBED HER arms against a sudden chill and slowly turned. *Just a little draft,* she reassured herself as she bumped the thermostat up a few degrees. But tonight she'd felt it in several rooms on the main floor, not just near the door to the cellar stairs, where she usually felt it. Yet the weather was clear, cold and still.

The creaks and groans of the old house reflected the below-zero temperature outside and heat indoors, as the house settled in for the night. Sometimes, it sounded for all the world as if someone were upstairs. *Walking.*

A feeling of inestimable sadness swept over her— something so real, so palpable, that it was almost frightening in its intensity.

"I need more sleep," she muttered as she flipped off the kitchen lights and walked to the parlor with a novel in her hand.

Sleep, and a little company.

But Badger had disappeared into one of his

hiding places, and Grant had taken Sadie for the day…though surely he'd be driving up any minute to bring her back.

For all that Jill had given him a hard time about the dog, Sadie was welcome company in this big old house, and it seemed terribly lonely without her.

In the parlor, Jill paced to the window and peered out into the darkness toward the lane, but could see only her reflection in the glass. Chastising herself for her foolishness, she snuggled into a woolen afghan on the sofa with her novel, and started on Chapter One.

After page two she glanced out the window again. After page three, she resisted the urge to pace the floor.

On page four, she felt that bone-chilling cold again. *Either my imagination, or the start of influenza,* she thought grimly, forcing herself to read on.

Relief poured through her when she saw the glow of headlights arc across the room. *Finally.*

A few minutes later she heard footsteps on the front porch. After checking through the peephole in the door, she opened it wide. Sadie bounded in, aquiver with excitement, her tail wagging furiously.

Grant hesitated for a second before stepping just inside the door. "Sorry to be so late. I got wrapped up in some things at the office, and one of my clients couldn't come until six."

"No problem." She tried to temper the obvious relief in her voice. "I could get you a cup of coffee, if you'd like."

"I should be going." Still, he stuffed his gloves in his jacket pockets as he searched her face. "You look pale. Is everything all right?"

"Of course. Never better." She waved toward the parlor. "I was just reading and must have lost track of time."

He glanced over her shoulder. "So that's where the infamous rocker is, right?"

She laughed lightly. "Yes, but it's been behaving since I mentioned it to you."

"You could just discard it, you know," he said as he walked over and rested his hand on the spindle back. He gave it a push and watched it rock back and forth. "Goodwill would take it if an antique store wouldn't, but I'd guess it's quite old." He looked at her. "If you took it to *Antiques Roadshow*, you might find that it's worth a hundred grand."

"It could pay off a good share of this place. But you know, it just seems to belong right there. Sometimes I wonder…" Embarrassed, she cleared her throat and bent down to rub Sadie behind the ears.

"What?"

"Nothing, really." Self-conscious, she laughed. "It's just that I sometimes think I can almost see the silhouette of a woman sitting right there, in that very same rocker…looking out the window day after day. Just my imagination."

"Think how old this place is—the late 1800s, or so we were told. Maybe what you saw was a woman waiting for her son to return from the war. Or her lover."

"My thoughts, too," she said before she caught his smile and realized he was only joking. "Nice, you brat." She smacked him on the back. But despite his cynicism, she felt herself relax for the first time in several hours. "I'm glad you came in, Grant. Are you sure about the coffee?"

He shook his head. "I'd like to use your phone, though, so I can check messages on my office answering machine. Someone—" he reached into his pocket, withdrew a mangled cell phone and frowned in Sadie's direction "—apparently thought this was a chew toy."

Sadie glanced back and forth between them, her tongue lolling and her tail thumping against the hardwood floor.

"I think she's telling us that it was a mistake, and she won't ever do it again," Jill said with a laugh. "Go ahead. You can have some privacy on the kitchen phone. There's a notebook and pen on the counter if you need them."

"By the way, I called on your patient yesterday afternoon."

"Patsy?"

"I wasn't able to talk very long. Her caregiver said hospice had upped her pain meds, and she was too woozy to make much sense. I promised to come back whenever they call me."

"Thank you. I'm afraid she doesn't have much time left."

He stared at the floor for a moment before meeting Jill's gaze. "She looks terrible. Her color is sallow and she's just skin and bones. And she's got those kids—" He swallowed hard. "It's just so damned unfair."

"I couldn't agree more." His voice sounded so raw and bleak that she wondered if he was thinking about the early years of their marriage. When they'd tried to have kids and couldn't. Or later, when he'd wanted to try every means possible, and she'd been too driven to succeed at her residency and new medical career.

They'd never really been on the same page for anything that truly mattered.

Jill moved back to the sofa and her book after Grant finally went into the kitchen. Sadie trotted over to sit beside her, resting her warm, furry head on Jill's lap. "You are one very special dog," Jill murmured. "I'm so glad to have you here."

With dogs, everything was so simple. You fed them, they loved you. But with people... Why was everything so very hard?

Grant appeared a few minutes later, his mouth a grim line. "I got the call I'd been waiting for, but there was another one, as well. It's probably nothing. I'm sure of it, in fact…but I'll report it to the police, and you should know."

She stared up at him. "A crank call?"

"Exactly. He didn't leave a name or number, and I'll bet there's nothing but Unknown on the caller ID at the office."

"A random message. One he could have left on anyone's phone?"

Grant gave a short laugh. "Unfortunately, no. Though few people are aware that Dad is out of town, so I don't know which of us was the target. That would have helped narrow the field a little. The guy promised 'retribution' of some sort."

"Did he say *how* he planned to exact this revenge?"

"Nope." Grant shrugged. "But I'm not too concerned."

"Did he say why?"

"No, he was too smart for that. We could track him down, if he had."

Jill hugged Sadie's neck. "Had any disgruntled clients lately?"

"I can think of several, but this could go back much further. Might not even be one of our clients. It could be someone a client sued, and that opens up a slew of other possibilities." He shook his head. "I wouldn't even know where to begin with all the clients Dad has seen over the years."

"I hope you'll be careful, Grant." He seemed nonchalant, but nervousness unsettled her stomach at the thought of him going out to his car in the darkness. Driving down that narrow, twisting lane. "Maybe you should stay here tonight."

His head shot up at that. "If you're worried about being alone, I'll stay, but he didn't mention anything about you."

"I was thinking about you going outside. What if he followed you?"

"I would've seen his headlights, especially if he'd turned up Bitter Hollow Road. No one else comes back here." Grant zipped his jacket. "You have your security system armed, right?"

She nodded.

"You also have Sadie, a land phone and your cell phone. But say the word, and I'll stay in the guest bedroom or down here on the sofa."

The offer was oh so tempting. Just having him here filled her with a sense of peace, but the idea of him staying all night brought it all back—the time when they'd slept warm and secure in each other's arms. When storms, and things that went bump in the night were an excuse to cuddle even closer.

But she was a big girl, and she certainly didn't need a babysitter. Or exquisitely compelling memories of exactly how good he was once the lights were turned low.

"I'm set—and I'm not worried, honest," she said briskly. "I was only thinking of you."

"Ninety-five percent of these callers hide behind the anonymity of a phone. They make threats they'd never have the balls to carry out."

"I know." She kept her voice light, nonchalant as she led him out. "You have a good night, you hear?"

But as she locked the door behind him and checked the security system one last time, his statistics started running through her brain.

Ninety-five percent. *But what about the other five?*

Uneasy, she whistled to Sadie and headed upstairs to bed, saying a long and heartfelt prayer for Grant's safety…and her own.

"WHY DO YOU do these things?" Mandy demanded, after cornering Ross at his locker following first-hour Spanish on Monday morning. "My friend Sara just told me what happened in there, and it isn't funny."

He stared into his locker. "Didn't say it was."

"You back-talked the teacher. Made fun of her class. How could you do that?"

"What are you, my mother?" He shot an angry glance at her. "Back off."

But she just stood there, not moving an inch. "I *like* you. You seem like a cool guy. A lot of other people would like you too, if you'd let them. And acting stupid in class isn't the way to start."

The teacher was a first-class jerk. She'd singled him out from day one, calling on him when he didn't volunteer, giving him a fish-eyed look if she heard a disruption in the class and didn't know who to blame.

He ducked his head, slammed the locker door with a resounding *clang* and shouldered his way through the crowd. First Mandy, and now he had to face Principal Travers and Aunt Grace. Again.

Only this was worse, because the guy was talking about useless stuff, like counseling. And next he'd probably suggest medication, like at the school back home. Fat chance of that.

Pills had been prescribed once before, at his mom's insistence, but he hadn't been the one who took them. He only had to look as far as her to see what some of those weird drugs could do.

HE MADE IT to the principal's office a couple minutes late. The secretary glanced pointedly at the clock on the wall and waved him on back. He dragged his feet.

He sure didn't need some principal or nosy counselor telling him why things didn't go well…he already knew that he scored high and failed to follow through.

Lack of focus, the last one had said. *Laziness.*

No motivation and low self-esteem, according to the counselor before that one. Self-centered. Rebellious.

At Travers's door, the murmur of voices and a burst of laughter made him pull to a halt.

He peered around the corner and there was Travers, leaning back in his chair with a big grin on his face, and Grace was telling him something that made him laugh again.

Her cheeks were pink and she almost looked like a teenager, the way she was smiling.

Grace and Principal Travers? They were so *old,* yet it almost looked like they were flirting. The whole idea was so…so *out there* that he could only stand by the door and gawk.

Travers chuckled at something else, then must have caught Ross out of the corner of his eye, because he rocked forward in his chair and beckoned for him to come in.

Feeling like an intruder at his own appointment, he nodded to Grace and dropped into the chair next to her.

She beamed at him and patted his knee. "Principal Travers and I are old schoolmates," she said. "And later, his wife became one of my dearest friends."

"The good old days," Travers said, still smiling. "But today we're here to talk about you, Ross. How do you think this week has gone?"

He slouched a little lower in his seat. "Okay, I guess."

"In what ways, do you think?"

He twitched a shoulder.

Travers used the old stay-silent-until-the-kid-blurts-something-out ploy, but Ross just studied the double knots on his shoelaces and counted off the seconds…truly at a loss for what to say.

"Our counselor isn't at school today, but she's done some checking. We didn't receive much information before you arrived, and we were curious as to how things have gone in the past." Travers flipped open a manila folder on his desk. "Looks like you've attended quite a number of schools…many of them inner city. I'd guess from the staffing ratio and tight budgets in those schools they didn't offer many accelerated classes or strong learning disability programs."

In most of them, an entire, overcrowded class had had to share just a few textbooks, and the teachers had barely managed to keep control.

"One of the schools gave you a lot of tests when you were eleven," Travers continued. "Fawnbrook, close to Chicago. Do you remember that school?"

"I was there half a year."

"What did you think of it?"

"It was all right, I guess." With clean, bright classrooms, shelves loaded with books and smaller classes, it had been the very best school of all. He'd almost cried when his mom had decided to move again.

Travers gave him a knowing look. "It was a good place. You would have done very well there, I think.

They started you in some extra, accelerated math and science classes, and also identified certain reading disabilities. You had a resource teacher there who was ready to help you a great deal."

Mrs. Posey. She'd seemed like a grandma right out of a storybook—kind, gentle, with twinkling blue eyes. He'd nearly cried over leaving her, too.

"I see some records that I don't agree with at all." Travers tapped a finger on the stack of papers in the folder. "Kids with learning disabilities are often frustrated in school. Sometimes they act out, because on a subconscious level, it feels better to be labeled a troublemaker than slow. One counselor was adamant about having Ritalin prescribed for you."

Grace frowned. "So what can you do for him here?"

"Fortunately, he's already been identified by Fawnbrook, and an IPP was started on him there—that's an individualized program plan for education—so we can update that and easily schedule him into a resource room. I think we can also challenge him more in the areas where he excels." He tapped an intercom. "Miss Kelly? See if Mrs. French is available for a few minutes. I have someone I'd like her to meet."

Ross's stomach was tied up in knots. He remembered some of the special classes at his old schools. Rooms full of disruptive BD kids, or the kids with severe physical and mental disabilities.

"I don't have any of those problems." He tried to

still the quaver in his voice. "I'm not different—not like that."

Travers braced an elbow on the arm of his chair and rested his chin in his palm. "I think you'll be surprised at some of the kids who spend time in the Resource Room. People with learning disabilities are often extremely bright. Given the right tools and a little extra support, the playing field is more level for them and they often surpass everyone else."

Grace covered one of Ross's hands with her own. "How soon can this happen?"

"This week. Mrs. French will be here in a minute, and she can fill you in. As for the accelerated classes, the third term starts in a few weeks. I'll talk to the teachers and see what might be a good fit, given that Ross is coming in midyear." Travers shifted his attention back to Ross. "You've had a tough situation, switching schools so often. I know it hasn't been anything you could control, but I'd like to talk to your mom, should she want you to leave here. If at all possible, it would be a great benefit if you could at least finish out the rest of high school in one place. Socially, as well as from an academic standpoint."

Still uneasy, Ross nodded. Changing schools sucked big time. Never being caught up, never knowing anyone, he'd drifted through school feeling like an alien. But this *resource* room sounded like just one more way he'd feel different, and alone.

At a soft rap on the door, he looked over and saw a pretty young teacher dressed in jeans and a bright red sweater.

"Mrs. French, I'd like you to meet Ross Villetti."

She smiled at him. "Would you like a tour of the classroom?"

Grace gave him an encouraging nod, and he had no choice but to follow the teacher down the hall like a sheep going to slaughter. Thankful, at least, that this was mid-hour and the halls were empty.

She chatted about the available services, then stopped at a door and ushered him in. "I think you know some of our students here this hour," she said. "Please, make yourself at home."

He took a deep breath and stepped inside, half afraid to survey the kids who were supposed to be problems, just like him—

And looked straight into the smiling eyes of Mandy Welbourne and two of her friends.

It hadn't been hard to come up with a new identity. He'd left Florida with credit cards obtained through identity theft, a forged driver's license and a car he'd actually paid for and registered under his new name. Once his boss at the welding shop agreed to cover for his absence—for a few hundred bucks— he was home free.

Even if he missed his next meeting with his

parole officer, it was unlikely anyone would come looking for him.

Ray studied his new haircut and glasses in the rearview mirror of the car and bared his teeth in a smile. He had time. He had a good cover. And his quarry was blissfully ignorant of his plans.

It was all about justice, really. And making sure people paid for the crimes they committed.

CHAPTER TEN

GRANT HIT ENTER on the computer keyboard, leaned back and smiled as the new program lit up the monitor.

He and Dad had talked about these software updates for months, and though Warren had agreed in theory, he'd never gotten around to taking the first step.

He'd gotten out of the hospital yesterday afternoon and was supposed to take a long vacation, but he'd probably show up any minute, anyway.

"Well, Dad," Grant said to the empty room, "when you come back to this office you'll finally be set to step into the twenty-first century, ready or not."

"Hey, Grant. I don't think anyone is here except me."

Surprised, he looked up and found Jill leaning against the door of his office with her arms folded. "I didn't hear you come in."

"I've been here for several minutes. You're just lucky I'm not that crazy caller you had. You might be tied to your chair by now."

He slipped the installation CD into its jewel case. "I'm probably at greater risk from all those high school students selling magazine subscriptions this week."

"Do they know you're a soft touch?"

He laughed. "I think they posted my name on a blackboard somewhere. I've tried to buy one subscription from each one, and when those magazines start flooding in there isn't going to be room for clients in the waiting room. Dad will be thrilled."

She came across the room and leaned over to peer at the screen. "Billable hours software? Now, that sounds exciting."

"It is, actually. Trying to keep accurate records isn't easy…but that's how we get paid, for the most part." He clicked the mouse to bring up the next screen. "It's a timekeeping application that lists the category of expense, the start and stop times and what I've done. I can print off copies if anyone questions what I've charged."

"Very cool. Is Warren going to figure this out?"

"I'll help him. He'd have a much bigger retirement fund if he'd kept better track all these years."

She rested a fingertip on one of the unopened software boxes on the desk. "And this?"

"Billing software."

"More exciting by the minute," she said dryly. "If it works well, let me know and I'll send Donna over to check it out."

Grant closed the program and pushed away from the desk. "You'd have to come along—or at least make sure she isn't armed. That woman *really* doesn't like me."

Jill lifted a brow. "No kidding. Honestly, she's more protective than a Doberman, and she's become a good friend as well."

And she was probably the one who'd been so quick to report his supposed transgressions last fall, though Grant didn't say it aloud. "Speaking of dogs, I didn't have time to pick up Sadie this morning. Will she be okay at home alone all day?"

"She's doing fine, so you won't need to dog-sit anymore." Jill reached into her purse and withdrew Grant's damaged cell phone. "You left this on my kitchen counter. And since you don't need to stop by the house, I thought I'd better drop it off. You might need this for…um…warranty replacement."

"Thanks, but I'm pretty sure there's a clause in the contract about dog damage." At the amusement in her eyes he felt a sudden tightening in his chest. God, he missed her. Despite everything that had made their separation necessary, he missed her.

"I need to drive down to Minocqua on Saturday to buy a new one," he added on an impulse. "I don't suppose you'd like to come along. We could have lunch, and stop at that great bookstore in town. On our way, we could even check out the antiques at The Mill, just for old times' sake."

"Two of my favorite places." She wavered, then visibly pulled back, her expression shuttered. "But it's probably not a good idea."

"Right. I forgot just how busy you are."

SHE'D REJECTED HIM so many times, he'd lost count.

Every time he'd broached starting a family— which meant more to him than…anything.

All the times he'd wanted to get away for weekends, but she'd refused because of her ironclad commitment to the hospital, or patients ready to deliver.

Other doctors could have covered for her—as she did for them—but she'd never been able to strike a balance between medicine and her personal life. Her refusal to come with him to Minocqua shouldn't have been a surprise.

Any observer would have said their relationship was over when they'd separated last fall, but somehow—despite the arguments and complete difference of opinion on almost everything—he'd apparently held on to hope.

Now, he finally understood.

His friends had told him it was time to move on. He should have already.

And dammit, he was doing it now and he wasn't looking back.

He stuffed a folder into the bank of file cabinets behind his desk and slammed it shut. After his last appointment at two o'clock, he'd be out of here for the day. Maybe he could even make it to Minocqua before the phone store closed at five, if he escaped before anyone else called or dropped in.

When the last client—a ninety-three-year-old man wanting to set up a revocable living trust—toddled in at two-thirty on the arm of his daughter, Grant dredged up a smile and ushered them in.

At five-fifteen, he groaned and rubbed a hand over his face, his ears still ringing from the contentious daughter's questions and the way she'd had to bellow everything into the old man's ear. He hadn't understood much of the proceedings anyway, so she'd repeated it all several times.

Then she'd been unhappy about some stipulations, and they'd had to start all over again.

Grant powered down the computer, glanced around and turned off the lights in his office. The phone rang as he reached for his jacket in the hall closet. *Damn.*

He sighed heavily, but retraced his steps and stood at his desk listening as the answering machine took the call.

From the first low, derisive laugh, he wished like hell he knew who was on the line. The caller ID screen read Unknown.

"I know you're still in the office—I can see the lights." The male voice dropped to a raspy growl. "So listen good. You made a mess of my life, and I'm returning the favor. Believe me, both you and that sweet little wife of yours are a lot more vulnerable than you think."

The connection ended with a soft click.

Grant spun around and raced to the front door, flung it open and scanned the street. Several cars passed by in opposite directions, the colors nearly indistinguishable in the dusk, beneath the rime of road salt and dried slush.

No one stood at the pay phone on the street corner.

He scanned the scattering of parked cars. No telltale cloud of exhaust from a car idling…waiting.

Then again, maybe the caller had driven by minutes ago, checked to see if the lights were on, then made the call from any number of public telephones around town.

Swearing under his breath, Grant called Jill to warn her, before dialing the sheriff's office to report it.

Then he barreled out the back door and headed for his car.

"YOU'VE GOT TO take this seriously," Grant insisted, pulling Jill into an empty waiting area of the hospital. "This guy sounds aggressive. And this time, he extended the threat to you."

Apparently, Grant thought she'd been too blasé over the phone, so he'd shown up at the hospital just after she'd started her rounds.

"So what am I supposed to do? I've got Sadie and Badger at home to take care of. I'm not just going to sit in town and cower. You said yourself that ninety-five percent of these callers are just hot air."

"That," he ground out, "was before he mentioned *you.*"

"I'm sorry, but I still have to go home." She jangled her keys in front of him. "I've got Mace on this key ring. I can take care of myself. And if I'm not at home with the security system—" she tapped the phone clipped to her belt "—I can call 911."

"Look, I called the sheriff, but this guy was smart enough to use a pay phone here in town. There's no way to identify him."

She crossed her arms and impatiently drummed her fingers against her sleeve. "So you have no idea who it is."

"I gave the sheriff a list of five clients who've been upset about one thing or another. He said he'd try to check them out. Unfortunately, crank calls aren't high on the list for such a small force, and there's no guarantee that he'll get to them any time soon." Grant scowled at her. "And as I said before, this could even be someone else…"

"What do you want me to do?"

"You shouldn't be alone."

"Grant," she bit out. "I'm *always* alone."

"Maybe you should stay at Dad's place."

"No."

"Or, I could stay in one of the spare rooms at Chapel Hill for a few nights."

He didn't look any happier about the idea than she felt, which made her answer easy. "No."

He growled something under his breath.

"Look, I'll ask the sheriff to cruise up my road now and then. Think about it. This guy takes ten seconds out of his life to make this threat, and we're supposed to totally change what we do?" She threw up her hands in frustration. "He could keep calling for weeks. Months. How long do we have to accommodate him?"

"Just until the sheriff has a chance to investigate."

"And a suspect is going to just blurt out that he made these calls, easily as that? I don't *think* so."

"Jill." Grant gently took her by the shoulders and turned her to face him. "I know we don't have a relationship anymore. But please, just do me this one favor."

He'd never take no for an answer. Back in the days of her residency and the late hours it entailed, he'd always been far more worried about her safety than she'd ever been. "One night. *Only.* And it should probably be at Chapel Hill, because of Sadie and Badger."

"Good." He gave her shoulders a squeeze before dropping his hands. "How long will you be?"

"An hour and a half, probably. Why?"

"I can follow you home." He glanced at his watch. "I'll take care of some errands and meet you here between seven and seven-thirty. If you aren't done, I'll wait. Deal?"

She managed a grudging nod, then watched as he strode down the hall toward the front entrance, and wished she'd refused.

JILL FINISHED HER hospital rounds at six-fifteen. Minutes later, her cell phone rang and when she picked up she heard Barb's frantic voice. "It's Patsy. Please, come quick."

Leaving a brief message for Grant at the front desk, she grabbed her coat and purse from her locker in the doctor's lounge and raced for her car.

Patsy had wanted her last days to be at the hospital, but had been delaying the move back. Hoping, Jill knew, that she had much more time.

Now, with three young children home from school and a frantic sister, the situation was probably everything Patsy had hoped to avoid.

Jill made it across town in minutes, pulled to a stop in front of the little house and ran to the door. Barb met her, her face tear-streaked and a wet ball of tissue in her hand.

"She's...gone," Barb said, sniffling. "It just happened so fast."

The house was quiet. Too quiet. "The children—where are they?"

Barb blew her nose and closed her eyes for a moment as fresh tears streamed down her face. "She's been in so much pain. Unbearable pain, even with the morphine. But this afternoon, she seemed comfortable, somehow—as if she'd moved past it all. I-it sounds insane, but I had this hope that she could even get b-better."

"The children?" Jill repeated gently. She moved to the bed and carefully checked for a pulse, then adjusted her stethoscope, already knowing the heart sounds would be absent. Patsy's pupils were dilated and fixed.

"She was so lucid this afternoon. She talked to the kids. Hugged them. Told them how much she loved them. As if…as if she *knew*." Barb drew in a shuddering breath. "She had me send them over to the neighbor's for an overnight a couple hours ago. Maybe an hour later she fell asleep, and I couldn't wake her…so I called you…but then I realized…"

"She slipped into a coma, Barb. We can be so thankful that she had such a gentle death." Jill set aside her stethoscope and gave the older woman a long hug. "At the end, she didn't suffer."

Jill waited with her until the unmarked funeral home van arrived to take the body, then helped her straighten up the living room.

"Do you have the number for the medical supply

company?" Jill said. "They'll come for the bed right away."

"I'll call them when they open tomorrow." Barb surveyed the room with reddened eyes. "I can't believe it's over. All the pain, and grief and worries—and now it's done."

"Did Grant get over here to take care of Patsy's last wishes?"

"He did. I-it's just hard to believe that this day has come." Her eyes filled with tears again. "I think I'll just stay here tonight and say my goodbyes."

"She was blessed to have such a loving sister." Jill gave Barb another hug, then stepped out into the crystalline night air.

It could be a record setter tonight. She shivered and held the collar of her coat tightly at her neck as she made her way down the slippery steps to the sidewalk and, beyond that, her car.

Filtered through the overhead branches of an old oak, the full moon cast gnarled shadows across the snow, and from somewhere nearby came the haunting cry of an owl.

Her hands were shaking with cold when she tapped in the code on her car door. Inside, she fumbled with the key. Tried to fit it into the ignition. Dropped it, and had to grope for it on the floor of the car.

She tried again. This time the key fit.

But the engine didn't roar to life. Had she left the lights on in her haste? Was it the starter?

Frustrated, she gripped the top of the steering wheel with both hands and rested her forehead against them before trying again.

Nothing.

She patted her bulky coat for the reassuring shape of her cell phone. Grant wouldn't be happy about her leaving the hospital, but if she left another message for him there, perhaps he'd come after her. For the price of a lecture she could at least get home.

She caught the flash of headlights in her rearview mirror.

Slowly. Ever so slowly, a car crept down the street.

Just someone coming home, taking care on the snowy street, she told herself. *Nothing more than that.*

It drew closer, a dark unidentifiable shape hidden behind blinding headlights. Closer yet. She twisted in her seat, trying to make out the model. Maybe it was Grant. She had left him that message....

The vehicle abruptly reversed.

Halted.

Then roared ahead, fishtailing in the snow and slamming her bumper with enough force to whiplash her head against the back of the seat and knock the phone out of her hand.

She automatically hit the brakes, but her car skidded ahead ten, fifteen feet.

The other vehicle had stopped a dozen feet behind, its lights still on bright. Waiting. *But for what?*

Frantic now, she laid a hand on the horn and scrambled desperately for her phone, her throat dry and her pulse racing, the blaring of the horn barely drowning out the thunder of her pulse.

Her fingertip touched the edge of the phone. She grasped it and struggled back up behind the wheel to find that the other car had pulled along-side, just inches away…its lights off and the driver hidden in shadow.

She hit the horn intermittently now. Long. Short. Long…until lights came on in several of the houses at the end of the block. Then porch lights. Someone lifted a shade and peered out.

And then another set of headlights topped the hill behind her.

The other car's motor roared and it took off.

Shivering more from fear than she had from the cold, she judged the distance back to Patsy's place, then double-checked her locks and debated running back to the house.

But Barb had appeared so exhausted…. Maybe she'd gone upstairs to lie down. Those house lights hadn't turned on in response to the car horn, and if she didn't hear Jill knock, it would be much safer to stay in the car. The other houses with lights on might be too far away.

And God only knew who might be in that approaching car.

Her heart in her throat, she punched in the speed dial number for the hospital....

It was still ringing when the second car pulled alongside hers, and the passenger window rolled down.

Grant.

Weak with relief, she sagged against the back of the car and closed her eyes.

"What in the hell are you doing out here alone?" he demanded. "You should have called me before you left."

She tried to smile but she was trembling too hard. "Y-you don't have a cell phone yet, remember? I did leave a message for you at the front desk of the h-hospital."

"Can you follow me?"

"I-it won't start."

Leaving his own car double-parked, he came around to her door, opened it and tried the key. "Battery," he announced. "I'll get my cables."

Five minutes later, he'd jump-started her car. After slamming both of the car hoods shut, he came back to her door with his jumper cables dangling from one hand.

"You didn't have a chance of going anywhere," he said, his face a grim mask. "Maybe it's a coincidence, but one of the connectors was loose."

"I doubt it was a coincidence. There was another car—just before you. He hit the back of my car and took off. Maybe it was your friend."

Grant pivoted and rounded the back of her car, then came back a second later. "The bumper took the brunt of it—I can't see any damage to the fenders or trunk in this light. You think it was an accident, or intentional?"

She managed a shaky laugh. "I'd say intentional."

"Are you all right?" When she nodded, he added, "Now this time, *listen.* Drive home and I'll follow, okay?"

She'd never liked taking orders. For most of her adult life she'd made it a point to ignore most of them, unless they were rephrased as a request.

But her battery was no accident.

Someone had lingered to watch, and then delivered a very clear message.

And letting Grant stay at Chapel Hill for the night now sounded like a very good idea, indeed.

CHAPTER ELEVEN

ON THE LONG drive home, images of Patsy had flashed through her thoughts. She grieved for the life lost far too young and for the children who would mourn their mother for years to come.

The frightening incident with that other car and the possibility that someone had tampered with her battery paled in comparison.

During med school and her residency she'd listened to the warnings about keeping distance between doctor and patient. Death happened, and getting too close led to burnout.

But it was still difficult to keep that distance with children and young adults, and this case had hit her especially hard. Even back at Chapel Hill, after she'd changed into sweats and thick wool socks, Jill couldn't stop shaking.

Grant called her to the kitchen.

The fragrance of hot coffee filled the room, along with buttered whole wheat toast and the omelettes he always used to make with sautéed onions, mushrooms and cheddar cheese.

He frowned at her approach. "You should have taken a good, hot bath. You're still chilled to the bone. This food can keep, if you'd rather warm up."

She eyed the table he'd set, and wished she had an appetite. He'd always been a far better cook than her. "I'm fine, really. I'll feel better after I eat, and this looks wonderful."

He sat across from her and polished off his own meal, then watched her push her food around her plate. "Maybe we'd better talk."

She managed a weak smile. "I'm just not as hungry as I thought, I guess."

"No surprise, with the night you had. I'm really sorry about Patsy, by the way. Knowing death is inevitable doesn't make it easier."

"Not for her family, certainly." She cradled her coffee cup in both hands, savoring its comforting warmth. "I feel sorry for her young kids. They'll grieve for her now, and at every big event in their lives."

"Sad business all the way around." He topped off her cup from the carafe he'd left on the table, then leaned back in his chair. "You sure didn't need any extra stress tonight."

She took a steadying breath. "That other car sure scared me."

"Did you catch the license? The make and model?"

"Are you kidding? It was dark. My windows were still frosted."

He reached across the table and took her cold hands in his. "It might have been my crank caller tonight, trying to intimidate you. I don't want to think what he might try next."

"We don't know it was the same guy. Could've been some teenagers, fooling around. And my battery could've been a coincidence." But she didn't really believe it. Not with her stomach still clenched in a cold knot of fear. Not with the darkness outside, and the vast acres of forest around the house providing a prowler ample cover.

Perhaps sensing her worry, Sadie lumbered heavily to her feet from her favorite spot over an old-fashioned heat grate in the floor and came to rest her head on Jill's lap.

Grant patted his waist for his absent cell phone. "Guess I'll need to use your phone," he said, pushing away from the table. He crossed to the kitchen counter and lifted the receiver. Frowned. "How long has your phone been out of order?"

"It hasn't been. Are you saying it's down again?" She sighed, then unclipped her cell and tossed it to him. "The wire goes through overhanging branches on the way up here. Ice, heavy snow or even a high wind can knock it down."

He cocked his head and listened for another

moment. "We'd better get this cell charged up, in case the phone's out all night."

He paced to the windows overlooking the backyard, punched in a series of numbers and spoke quietly into the phone, then searched several drawers until he found her phone charger.

"Randy's supposed to call me back." He plugged in the phone, then leaned against the counter and braced his hands on the edge. "He needs to take this seriously."

"He hasn't had a chance. The poor man just heard about it today, and he's got only one deputy."

"It shouldn't take long to check out five people. Hell, if our guy is one of them, just being questioned by the sheriff might be enough to knock some sense into him."

"Maybe, though he's hardly likely to admit to it. We won't know anything for sure."

Grant stood and stacked the plates. "I'll take care of the kitchen. Go take a nice, hot bath. You'll feel better, and if he wants to talk to you, I'll come knock on the door. Deal?"

"Just give me twenty minutes."

Upstairs, she ran the old claw-foot tub half full of steaming water, added her favorite scented oil and sank into it with pure gratitude. A single candle on the counter sent flickering light across the vintage black-and-white tiles on the wall.

Despite her insistence that she would be fine on her own, there was no denying that Grant's presence made her feel far more secure. If she'd come home alone, with the wind rattling the shutters and sleet still hitting the windows like BB shots, she would have jumped at every noise.

Now, she simply let the hot water soothe away her tension and exhaustion.

It would be so easy, to slip into old habits. Old expectations. Grant had once been her very own white knight and even now he easily stepped back into that role.

But it was impossible to go back, and they were both better off.

She just had to keep her distance and get through the next few months while he was in town.

By THE TIME she'd dressed, the electricity had faltered twice. It was out before she could reach her bedroom and the flashlight on her bedside table.

She heard footsteps coming up the open staircase. "Jill—are you okay?"

A moment later, a soft glow lit the hallway and Grant appeared with the pillar candle from the kitchen table.

By daylight, he was a rugged, appealing man. By candlelight, he loomed even taller, like a dark and dangerous baron straight out of some Gothic novel, the planes and hollows of his face cast in mysterious shadows.

He held the candle higher, providing enough illumination for her to find the flashlight and light the three-wick bayberry candle on the bureau. "The sheriff called me back a few minutes ago. He says he'll question the people on my list within the next few days. He'll also have his deputy pass this way at least once every night until we get this settled."

She'd nearly fallen asleep in the tub. She'd felt cozy and warm in her burgundy sweats and thick wool socks, but at the reminder of the danger, tension assaulted her again. "Good, then. Everything should be fine if you don't want to stay after all…"

"Are you kidding?"

"No, I—"

"Sadie has been outside for the last time tonight, and I've already gathered some blankets." His mouth hardened. "I'm not after anything, if that's what you're thinking. I'll sleep in the parlor."

Embarrassed, she managed a smile. "I didn't mean that at all. You've already been more than kind, and I just don't want you to bother. But if you *are* staying, you know there are several bedrooms up here that would be a lot more comfortable than that sofa."

"You should be down there, too. If the electricity doesn't come back on you're going to be cold up here. At least there's the fireplace."

"I've got two down comforters and a quilt, because it's always cold up here. I'll be fine."

"Whatever. Good night, Jill." He turned and disappeared down the dark hallway, the weak glow of his candle fading as he went downstairs.

She set the flashlight within reach on the bedside table, extinguished the candle and crawled under the heavy blankets. "Good night," she whispered, long after the house fell silent.

But instead of drifting off, images of a dying woman and unseen prowlers filled her thoughts, and she knew that sleep would elude her.

NEEDLES OF SLEET rattled the windows. The wind sent eerie keening sounds through the rafters, and something rustled—probably papers disturbed by a draft—in the attic above her room.

Badger appeared soundlessly, suddenly inches away from her face, his luminous gold eyes peering at her and his whiskers tickling her cheek. He curled up against her for a few minutes, his soft, heavy body a welcome source of warmth, and then abruptly leaped off the bed and disappeared. Off again on his nightly patrol duty.

After that, she'd watched the digital numbers on the bedside clock radio, running on its battery backup, drag minute by minute from midnight, to one o'clock.... Even now the numbers mocked her. *One-thirty.*

If she'd been home alone, she might have gone downstairs to light the old-fashioned kerosene lantern in the kitchen and read a few chapters just to while away the time.

But the stairs would creak at her descent. Grant would undoubtedly wake up, and that was hardly fair, given that he'd probably had a hard time falling asleep, too.

Then again—

A loud *crack* exploded just outside her window. Glass shards exploded into the room, rattling across the hardwood floor and raining onto her bed.

Stifling a cry, she ducked under the comforter for protection, her heart pounding.

Grant thundered up the stairs. "Jill! Are you okay?" He shoved her door and it banged open against the wall. "Good God!"

She cautiously pushed the blankets back, wary of the broken glass. "W-what happened?"

Grant stood in the doorway, sweeping the flashlight around the room, then settling it on the window. A broken tree limb protruded into the room.

"Stay there," he ordered. "I'll find you some shoes."

He crunched across the floor, angling the flashlight until he found the pair of sneakers she'd left next to the bureau. Glass tinkled to the floor as he shook them out, then tossed them aside. With a growl of impatience he opened the closet door and retrieved a pair of loafers.

"I'll hang a blanket across the window for the night, and we can just close this bedroom door," he said, handing her the loafers and a heavy robe he'd grabbed from a hook on the closet door. "We'll get someone up here tomorrow to repair this."

She carefully shook the glass from the comforter and folded the blankets back, slipping into the shoes. "I definitely wasn't expecting *this*," she said, grabbing her own flashlight.

He gently took her shoulders and searched her face. "Thank God your bed wasn't any closer to the window. Did you get cut anywhere? Are you bleeding?"

"Not that I can tell." An icy gust of wind blew through the broken window and she shivered. "What about downstairs—any damage?"

"I didn't hear any windows break. Other than that, we'll need to wait till morning to check the exterior."

"And Sadie?"

"I think she hid under the dining room table." He laughed. "She's a very brave girl."

"I don't blame her a bit." Jill shivered. "That fireplace sounds appealing to me right now."

"Let's get you settled down there, and then I'll come back up and take care of this." A corner of his mouth lifted in a wry smile. "At least we can safely say that this was Mother Nature's doing and not our stalker."

"Definitely a comfort," she replied with a shaky laugh.

They each took a stack of blankets from the linen closet on the way down to the parlor, where a single candle burned on the mantel of the fireplace. The downstairs felt chilly, too, but in a few minutes he built a fire with the wood stacked in the brass log holder. "Do you still keep extra firewood on the back porch?"

"There isn't much left, but it ought to be dry, anyway."

He walked a few steps away, then turned back and pulled her close. "Thank God you're all right," he murmured against her ear. "When I heard that crash…"

His voice trailed off as he tightened his embrace for a moment, then released her. "Eventful night, I guess." His voice husky, he took a step away. "Stay here. I'll be back in a minute."

She pulled an afghan around her shoulders and stayed by the fire, thankful for its radiant heat and the mesmerizing flicker of the flames.

Grant reappeared with a few more logs, which he stacked next to the fireplace. Straightening, he dusted his hands off and leaned one arm against the mantel to stare into the flames. "I got the last of your firewood."

"Rafe Hollister was supposed to deliver more yesterday, but he didn't show up. Wouldn't you know? Perfect timing."

"I also called the power company to see if it would be worth going to Dad's house, but the electricity is out all the way to the south edge of town." He looked over his shoulder at her. "I checked outside, too. You've lost a couple of trees in this wind. I think one is blocking the drive, so we won't be going anywhere for a while at any rate."

"Luckily I don't have any pregnant moms ready to deliver." She stood and stretched. "I can take the floor, if you want the sofa."

He chuckled. "I was just going to say the same thing."

Their eyes met.

"It's going to be cold, either way," she murmured.

"We could consolidate—and use half the blankets on the floor, the other half as a cover."

"Right." They'd certainly shared a bed during that last month of their marriage without ever coming close to touching each other. Her on one side of the bed, him with his back to her on the other. The chasm of silence and anger between them had been more impassable than any physical barrier. "Good plan."

They settled in, back-to-back, each at the far edge of the makeshift bed. But somehow, during the night, through the shifts and adjustments of trying to get comfortable and stay warm, she awoke to find herself nestled against his chest with his arm draped over her.

And a few minutes later, when he nuzzled the back of her neck, she sighed with pleasure and melted against him. Although the fire had faded to embers, which glowed with little heat, the room seemed to grow warmer.

He raised up on one elbow and looked down at her, his face sculpted by the faint light, his sensual mouth curving into a provocative smile. "Imagine this," he murmured. "You. Me. In this house again…and not at war."

She could read the desire in his smoky gaze, and she could hear it in the deep timbre of his voice.

"Not exactly at war," she said carefully. "Just separate."

He nibbled her ear, his breath hot and minty against her sensitive neck.

"Permanently separate," she amended. "This…this situation is just temporary. Because of the cold."

"Right." His voice dropped another octave. "But you know the rumors weren't true—I was never, ever unfaithful to you."

She shivered with anticipation as his large, warm hand found bare flesh below the hem of her fleecy top and slid slowly, ever so slowly upward, until his thumb grazed the soft undercurve of her breast.

She could have moved away; grabbed a blanket and found a spot across the room. But it felt so warm, so right, pressed against his hard-muscled chest. She shifted a little and looked up at him. Intended to tell him to stop.

But when his eyes locked on hers, she felt every

last protest melt away. This was Grant. The man she'd loved for so long…a man she'd slept with for years. And suddenly, after a night of facing the enormity of death and an unknown stalker, all that mattered was this moment and the need to feel Grant's mouth on hers.

The need to feel alive, and safe, and to lose herself.

She brushed her fingertips across his mouth, then curved her hand around his neck and smiled. "I think," she whispered, "that we still have protection in the bathroom cabinet upstairs."

He lowered his mouth to hers. His kiss was long, slow. Deep. A kiss of promise, of such intense, searching need that her heart quickened and everything melted away into liquid heat.

He levered himself away from her. "I'll be back," he growled.

He disappeared into the darkness, leaving her even more cold and bereft, but a moment later he returned and slid beneath the piles of blankets. He brushed a kiss against her lips, then pulled back. "If you've changed your mind, just say so," he said softly.

Maybe she'd regret it later, but she could no more have refused him than she could've stopped her own heart.

"I need you," she whispered. "Here. Now."

And until dawn, he fulfilled her every wish.

CHAPTER TWELVE

GRACE STAMPED THE snow off her boots, stepped into the entryway and took them off. "Four more inches and even bigger drifts now," she grumbled, wiggling her icy toes. "I think we're heading for a record this year."

"Just what we always wanted, right?" Jill helped her out of her coat. "What brings you out in this weather?"

"You called the hospital and said you wouldn't be in today. I was worried, what with you being up here alone and all, so I thought I'd better stop by after work."

"The snowplow didn't make it up the lane until after one o'clock, and then the tree-removal crew had to clear the lane before the plow could come the rest of the way." Jill laughed. "Coordinating them was like trying to set up surgery with a specific anesthesiologist—everyone's schedule is different."

"I saw the stack of logs out there. You must have lost a big tree."

"Two, and one of them hit the house." Jill flipped on the switch lighting the entry. "Luckily, Grant has a client who's a carpenter, and he got the guy to come out as soon as the road was clear. He left just a few minutes ago. I didn't even have electricity until almost eleven. Luckily, the pipes didn't freeze."

"Your phone still isn't working, and you didn't answer your cell. I tried a couple times."

"I must have left the cell phone upstairs." Jill stepped aside. "Would you like a cup of coffee?"

Grace nodded and followed her down the hall to the kitchen. "So how bad is the house?"

Jill poured two cups of coffee and set them on the kitchen table with a plate of cookies. "A broken window in the master bedroom, and damage to the frame itself. The carpenter covered and insulated it today, but he has to custom order a replacement. There was also some water damage in the attic just above my room."

"That's a shame." Grace sipped at her coffee, thankful for the warmth of the cup in her hands. "Must've been a frightening night, here all alone like that."

"I wasn't exactly alone." A faint pink rose in Jill's cheeks. "I mean, it wasn't intentional, but…"

No wonder Jill seemed so embarrassed and edgy. "Well, I always figured you two would work things out someday."

"No—it's not like that." Jill looked away. "I was upset after going to Patsy Halliday's home last night.

Grant came out to keep me company, but the weather turned bad and he couldn't leave."

"I heard that she passed away. One of her friends at the hospital thought the funeral would be on Saturday."

"If you're planning to go, maybe we can go together." Though she was dressed warmly in beige woolen slacks and a heavy Nordic sweater, Jill shivered. "I didn't realize last summer just how drafty this place is."

"Drafty? Feels warm as toast in here to me." Grace frowned. "You aren't getting sick, are you?"

Jill shook her head. "Just my imagination, probably." She bit her lower lip. "You've been here all your life, right? Do you know anything about this place? Its history?"

Well, that was certainly a loaded question. Grace hesitated, uncertain of just how much to say. A grown woman smart enough for a medical degree surely wouldn't be spooked by a few old stories, but still...

"Really, I'd like to know." Her tone nonchalant, Jill added, "Entertain me."

"Nothing ever happened here that made headline news, certainly, so don't worry about that. The place was empty for many years, actually...until some people from Indianapolis decided to start a bed-and-breakfast. They sank a fortune into new wiring, new plumbing—everything to bring it up to code. Never got beyond that, though. They went through a bitter divorce and had to put the place up for sale. It stayed empty for about three years after that, until you and Grant came along."

"That's not too reassuring. No one else wanted it but us?" Jill toyed with her coffee cup. "You'd think a lot of people would've loved this location."

"Just takes a certain kind of person to appreciate it, I guess." Actually, Ellen Dolby—the Realtor—had talked to Grace privately about how many eager buyers had taken one brief look, and then had been in a hurry to leave.

Some had complained about eerie sounds or a strange rush of air inside, though Ellen said she'd never noticed a thing. Some clients had barely stepped past the front door.

All of that, Grace figured, was sheer nonsense.

"What about way back? Are there any old tales?" Jill smiled over the rim of her cup. "I swear, I don't believe in the supernatural. I know it doesn't exist. But sometimes, I get the oddest feelings in this place. A sudden chill. Deep sadness. And I don't think anyone feels it but me."

Grace shifted uncomfortably. If Jill felt it, too, maybe there *was* something beyond imagination— and that possibility made her shudder. "You know how stories change over the years. This one could be so far from the actual history that it's just a fairy tale…"

Jill leaned forward. "Go on."

"People say this house was started by a young man for his fiancée. He joined the union near the end of the Civil War and was killed in one of the last battles—Fort Fisher, I think. Back when I was a kid, the town librarian found his name on the death rolls."

"How sad."

"The fiancée—Faye Williston—slowly finished the house, then pined for him the rest of her days. She lived into her eighties, but people never saw her in town."

A shadow crossed Jill's face. "Go on."

"There were…a number of owners after she died."

"And?"

Grace cleared her throat. "I know you aren't into *woo-woo* stuff, and neither am I. This is just hearsay. Probably embellished over the years."

Jill raised a brow. "Mass murderers? Bodies in the basement?"

"Good heavens, of course not. The first buyer committed suicide during the Wall Street Crash of 1929. All the rest supposedly ended up divorced, bankrupt or in family tragedies. People said it was as if…"

"Please." Jill rolled her eyes. "Not a 'curse.'"

"Well, I don't believe it, either." Grace took a last sip of coffee. "I shouldn't repeat such nonsense."

"Everyone dies sooner or later, and all too many divorce. Nothing unusual in that."

"Absolutely." Relieved, Grace smiled. Skipping lightly over *where* those tragedies had occurred had been a good decision, since the poor girl now lived in the house alone. Who needed bad dreams? And there couldn't be any truth to the old stories about how the house brought bad luck to its owners. "Guess I'd better get moving. Ross will be home from school soon."

"How's he doing?"

"Much better this week. He seems to have made a few friends, and I think the resource class will help him a lot."

"And the principal?" Jill teased.

"We met with him Monday." Grace dredged up a bright smile. "Once Ross is on the right track, I'm sure I won't see Travers at all."

There'd be only the chance hello in the grocery store, or casual wave on the street. Just as it had been since high school, when he'd been head over heels in love with a cheerleader, and Grace—dumpy, plain, ordinary Grace—had watched him from afar.

JILL WAVED GOODBYE, then locked the door behind her and leaned against it, her eyes closed.

It had been an exhausting day—after one completely sleepless and exhausting night.

What had she been thinking? She felt her face burn as she wondered about what Grant thought of her now. *Pathetic. Needy. Desperate.*

And weak, after she'd fallen apart over a patient and some creep who'd made a few stupid phone calls.

Totally pathetic.

No wonder Grant had followed her home and stayed the night. He'd probably figured she was on the verge of a mental breakdown and, in his usual white-knight fashion, figured he should be there to pick up the pieces.

And he'd also probably figured that, with a few trite words about his faithfulness, she'd melt like butter. Then, just before leaving this afternoon, he'd had the audacity to tell her that making love had been a *big* mistake.

Which added humiliation to the embarrassment, and made her want to scream in frustration.

As if she'd even *consider* going for Round 2.

The good thing was that he'd left the moment the lane was cleared. The bad thing was that he'd probably be back, assuming his "protector" role all over again...but with some sort of patronizing comment about keeping their distance.

Grinding her teeth, she pushed aside the crates of damp papers and water-damaged books she'd brought down from the attic.

She would go to the hospital to do her rounds. She would call Grant and tell him not to come over tonight. And then she would drive home and get to bed early—and forget that last night ever happened.

GRANT PACED HIS office, wishing Monday were *over*. Two of the last clients—elderly friends of his father—had both droned on about their health before buckling down to business.

The latest appointment, a custody battle heating up between two obnoxious parents who never should have had kids in the first place, had set his teeth on age.

And now sweet little Jennibell Perkins was due in five minutes. A former home economics teacher and as prim and proper as the Queen Mother, she'd given him a lecture on cruciferous vegetables when she'd come in the week before to discuss her plans for a living trust. Today she was planning to sign the papers, but he didn't even want to guess her new agenda. If it involved anything green he was going to plead indigestion and end her appointment early.

The sooner he got out to Jill's place again, the better.

After leaving her house Wednesday afternoon he'd worked at the office until almost eleven, catching up on everything he'd missed earlier in the day. The next morning he'd been on the road to Kendrick by six to prepare for a court hearing, and then there'd been a number of his Kendrick clients to see.

He'd tried calling her, but she'd been cold, dismissive…absolutely refusing to discuss what had happened between them on Wednesday night.

By the time he'd gotten back to Blackberry Hill Friday night he'd been so anxious over Jill's safety that he'd gone straight to Chapel Hill. And she'd practically slammed the door in his face.

She'd had a few days to cool down. She was a reasonable, intelligent woman. And at the very least, they needed to communicate in case there were any more threats to her safety.

At exactly one minute before four, Jennibell marched smartly into the office. Barely five feet tall, she moved like a soldier and he suspected she'd done her share of knuckle-rapping with a ruler in her day. She certainly brooked no nonsense now.

"Well, Mr. Edwards. Have you got your work done for me? Is it complete?"

"Yes, ma'am. Come on back to my office and we can go over it."

"Now, we discussed this before, correct?"

"Yes, ma'am."

"And you wrote everything up just as I required?"

"Yes, ma'am."

"Then what is there to discuss?"

"Well, I thought—"

"I remember everything very well." She swept past him and took a seat in front of his desk. "Let me check it over to make sure you got it right, and then I'll sign and be on my way."

Smothering a laugh, he dutifully followed her into the office and handed her the document, then settled in his own chair, half tempted to give her a red pen.

After propping her reading glasses on her nose she read each line slowly, tracing it with a gnarled finger, then pinned him with her stern gaze. "This looks exactly right."

"I'm certainly glad to hear it." He picked up the phone and dialed the insurance company secretary next door, who'd often served as a signatory witness if Doretta was out of the office. "Mina will be here in a minute or two so you can sign and be on your way."

Her brows drew together. "You looked stressed, young man. Do you get enough sleep?"

"Uh, yes, ma'am."

"Eight hours, every night? Your body needs that time for rest and rejuvenation, you know. Without it…"

He smiled and nodded as she launched into her sleep lecture, though his thoughts drifted back to the court case in Kendrick and then to Jill. She'd be done at the clinic a little after five, and then she usually did rounds at the hospital. If he caught her at, say, six-thirty, maybe they could just meet for a quiet dinner in neutral territory. The supper club over on Lake William, maybe…or…

"…don't you agree?" Jennibell rapped her knuckles sharply on his desk, startling him out of his reverie. Her eyes narrowed. "Or did you hear a word I said?"

"Yes…you're absolutely right. And I'm going to follow your advice tonight."

Appearing mollified, she gave Mina a tight smile

as the younger woman walked in. In a few minutes, both of them were gone and Grant leaned back in his chair with a sigh of relief.

Stressed? Jennibell was right. And he hadn't been sleeping well, either. Not since he'd spent the night at Jill's. She'd been on his mind ever since and he hadn't been able to stop the flood of memories that assailed him the moment his head hit the pillow every night.

If he just had a chance to talk to her, he could straighten it out and he'd be fine.

Perfectly, absolutely fine.

GRANT STOPPED JILL as she headed out the employee entrance of the hospital, expecting that she would coolly dismiss him and walk on past.

She shocked the hell out of him by grabbing his arm and steering him back inside to the doctor's lounge a few doors down the hall.

It was empty, thank God, because she looked as if she had a lot on her mind.

"Nice evening," he said mildly, propping a hip against the counter along the back wall. He gestured toward the double-burner coffee machine. "Want any?"

She shook her head. "We need to talk."

"How about dinner? We could talk there."

"No thanks." She paced the room, then wheeled

around to look at him, her arms folded. "Look, we made a mistake last Wednesday night. *As* you so kindly pointed out when you left."

He winced.

"You said, before the…big event…that you wanted me to know that you'd never been unfaithful to me. As if you thought that information was the key to my bedroom."

"I wasn't. I mean, I didn't." He faltered to a stop, all too aware that he could face down other attorneys in court, handle difficult witnesses and make a presentable showing in front of a judge, but with Jill, he might as well throw in the towel. He lowered his voice and spoke slowly. "I was not unfaithful to you."

"But when I asked you last fall, you were furious. You packed up your bags and walked out the door."

"Your lack of trust was the last straw. Without trust, we had nothing left."

"And for me, lack of communication was the final straw. There were a hundred rumors flying around this town. People who'd seen you meeting with that woman at a café in another town. People who saw her go into your office late at night. All I wanted was to talk about it."

"I'd already told you. How many times would it have taken?"

"That was different—when you came in at three in the morning."

"And if I'd given you my word again?"

A faint smile curved her generous mouth, but didn't reach her eyes. "We'd probably still be where we are today. But at least there wouldn't have been as much anger. We're two educated, intelligent people. We should have been able to handle this much better, don't you think?"

"So…it's entirely my fault, then."

Her shoulders sagged. "No. It was mostly mine. I always knew how much you wanted kids. I couldn't think of anything beyond establishing a practice. Anything else would've…"

"Gotten in the way?" He shook his head. "I was no better, Jill. I placed just as high a priority on my own career."

"And then when I got pregnant in the middle of it all, and miscarried…"

"That was a terrible time for both of us."

He started to move toward her, but she held up a hand. "Patsy's funeral Saturday made me realize how important it is to make priorities in your life. One of mine is to own up to my mistakes." She extended her hand. "We were wrong for each other, but I'd like to be friends. Truce?"

"Friends?" He looked down at her hand, then walked to the door and braced an arm against the frame. "No, I really don't want that at all."

And then he walked away without looking back.

CHAPTER THIRTEEN

ROSS LEANED CLOSER to Grace and, with one eye on the door of the principal's office, he lowered his voice. "I don't think we're gonna need these meetings again."

Grace beamed at him and patted his leg—something he'd once resented, because it made him feel like a little kid. But for an old lady, she was still pretty cool.

"I think you're right," she whispered back. "I had a call just the other day from Mrs. French. She said you're really settling in, and you were a great help with one of the other—"

Principal Travers stuck his head around the door. "Sorry to keep you two waiting. It'll be just another couple minutes."

He disappeared, and Grace winked at Ross. "I'm proud of you."

Proud of you. Ross tried to remember when he'd last heard *those* words. It sure hadn't been in recent history.

He mentally ticked off the remaining months of school here. From the second of March to the fourth of June, just three months. When he'd first arrived, summer had seemed like an eternity away. Now, the days were flying past in a blur. Too fast.

Grace had set him up with some of her friends for ice fishing, and that was sweet. And this weekend, a family next door was taking him snowmobiling. That sounded even better.

Back at home, he'd have a TV and an empty apartment to look forward to, because his mom was always gone.

Travers walked in and sat behind his desk. He folded his hands and met Ross's gaze squarely. "It's been a week and a half. I think you had some reservations about the resource room, so I wanted to touch base with you. How are things going?"

The guy had a way of looking at you that made you feel important. Like you *mattered* to him. Ross sat up straighter. "Good."

The guy smiled. "Tell me about it."

"French, er, Mrs. French is pretty cool. She helps me figure out my homework. Especially language arts."

"Your math teacher says you're gifted in his area and he believes you should be in an accelerated class next term. With help, you could catch up with the kids on the faster track, so you can get into calculus by your senior year. What do you think about that?"

"Good, I guess."

"Have you heard from your mother? Do you know yet where you'll be next fall?"

He shrugged. One call, during the whole three weeks since she'd announced she was getting married, and she'd been too rushed to talk more than a few minutes.

Travers glanced at Grace, and she lifted her hands, palms up. "Ross is certainly welcome to stay, but I haven't talked to Ashley since she brought him up here."

"We'll have him go ahead and register for fall classes when the time comes up this spring. That way he'll be covered."

Ross watched them with interest. Travers seemed to lean forward more when he talked to her, and his easy grin widened. And Aunt Grace—her cheeks got pink and she actually got *flustered*.

When Travers had to excuse himself to talk to someone at the front desk, Ross said, "I think he has the hots for you, Aunt Grace."

"Ross!"

"I mean it. You oughta do something about it. Like, ask him out or something."

"Be still!" she whispered as they heard Travers's footsteps coming down the hall.

"I'm telling you, he *does*. Go for it!" When Travers appeared at the door, Ross gave him an innocent look. "Can I go? I need to finish my math homework in study hall."

"Sure. I'm glad things are working out for you here, Ross. Come to see me anytime."

Travers shook his hand and, as Ross shouldered his backpack and started down the hall, he heard the two of them talking.

It was sort of weird. Yet both of them were old, and it had to be lonely getting older by yourself. If Ross had to leave this summer, at least Aunt Grace would have someone to talk to.

"You LEAD ONE amazing life," Jill muttered to herself as she took off her coat and hung it in the closet. "*Sooo* exciting."

Sadie nuzzled her arm. She bent to give the dog a hug, then let her out the front door to do her business.

Jill's gaze fell on the old marble-topped, gate-legged table in the entryway. Another one of the treasures she'd found in the attic, it was the perfect size for an arrangement of dried flowers and the small Staffordshire bowl she put her car keys in.

Except now, an old book lay next to the flowers. It certainly hadn't been there when she'd left for work this morning. A ledger of some sort, with a crumbling leather cover and gilt-edged pages mostly worn to gray. Its musty scent tickled her nose.

She shivered, imagining how ghostly hands

might have placed it here… Then she chuckled. *Ridiculous idea.*

Grant had probably come back to inspect the storm damage and found the book in the attic. Or maybe the carpenter had brought it down. "Grow up," she muttered.

Sadie, not much of an outside dog, was already scratching at the door. "Come on in, you silly girl," Jill said, opening the door wide.

Sadie bounded in, her tail wagging. It really took so little to make that dog happy, Jill mused as she gingerly picked up the book and took it to the kitchen. Setting it aside, she made herself a cup of coffee and then settled at the table.

The dog dropped in front of her, her eager eyes watching every move as Jill carefully lifted the cover of the journal and tried to make out the spidery script.

"I know you want your dog cookies, but this is really amazing," Jill murmured. "How strange. I think I've just found Faye."

Unimpressed, Sadie thumped her tail against the floor, her tongue lolling in anticipation. Jill reached behind herself, blindly groping for the jar, and withdrew several dog treats, her eyes riveted to the first page of the volume in her other hand.

She tossed the treats in the air and Sadie caught one on the fly, then scrambled across the floor for the others.

The book was slightly damp, its fragile pages

almost translucent. In places, the ink was blurred from moisture.

My Journal. Written in my Hand. Begun August 2, 1864.

Jill held her breath and carefully, slowly, tried to separate the first page from the second. The fragile paper gave way beneath her fingertips and she immediately released it, disappointed.

How strange it was that this book could have been in this house all these years…through so many owners…and suddenly here it was. Yet now, its contents might be lost forever.

Then again…

She turned to the computer she'd set up in a corner of the kitchen and logged on to the Internet to do a quick search on book preservation related to water damage.

The method requiring a hair dryer sounded faster, but the longer route seemed safer. She took the old book to the end of the kitchen counter, stood it on end and opened it enough to gently fan the pages without forcing any of the pages apart.

With luck, the reference was correct and the pages would separate when dry. And maybe then she could discover the reasons a woman had dedicated her life to this house. And why it had been filled with sadness ever since.

She idly toyed with her cell phone, then speed-dialed Grant to ask about the appearance of the journal. He'd been busy at his office all day, and he hadn't been back to the house. Her heart pounding, she phoned the carpenter, who took offense at her question. "I didn't see any book, lady. I didn't get into your things, and I sure as hell didn't bring anything downstairs from the attic."

And no one else had been in the house all day.

GRACE STOOD IN the frozen foods section of the grocery store reading the nutritional content label on a package. Out of the corner of her eye, she could see Dan at the other end of the aisle in front of an array of frozen vegetables. He was clearly perplexed.

Go for it, Ross had said, with his infinite, fifteen-year-old's wisdom.

But the concept of "going for it" and actually making that first, terrifying move…. She could manage her nurses. Meet a budget. Handle triage after a pileup on the interstate. But when it came to Dan Travers, her arthritic knees still turned to jelly. And that, she decided, was pathetic.

Firming her jaw, she put the frozen package in her cart—not even sure what it was—and wheeled down to the end of the aisle. "Hi, Dan."

He turned around with a look of surprise that softened into one of his deep-dimpled smiles. "Hey, Grace. I was hoping someone might come along."

He held up two packages of frozen hash browns.

"Leah always made the most wonderful hash brown casserole for holidays. I've been so hungry for it that I finally found her recipe. But now I'm not sure what to buy." His expression turned sheepish. "There are yellow onions, white ones or purple ones, and something called Vidalia, whatever that is. There must be sixteen kinds of frozen potatoes in here...and some of her directions weren't all that clear. Buttered bread crumbs? How many? And how in the world do you butter crumbs?"

"Leah and I used the same recipe," Grace said. She tapped the bag of shredded hash browns. "Buy this package. The yellow or the white onions are fine. You make the crumbs by whirling the bread in your food processor and then lightly fluffing them with a fork as you add your melted butter."

She hesitated. "If you'd like, I'd be happy to bring you a nine-by-thirteen pan of that recipe, or...maybe you could come over for supper sometime."

She expected him to accept the casserole but find an excuse to decline the dinner. Since his wife's death he hadn't been seen around town with another woman, as far as Grace knew. When he eventually did decide to see someone, she knew he'd find a trim, classy gal who played golf and put on elegant parties.

But instead of searching for an excuse, he nodded and his smile widened. "That sounds wonderful. Would you be willing to come to my place? We could make dinner together, and you could show me what to do."

"Of course," she said faintly.

"Tomorrow?" His eagerness faltered. "I guess that was rather rude, assuming you'd be free at such short notice on a Saturday night. I guess I'm too accustomed to being alone."

What had first seemed like a bid for a cooking lesson now seemed like just a little more than that, and her heart lifted. "I'm free, and I'll be there. Say, five o'clock?"

"Perfect. I'll pick up some T-bones, if you'd like that?"

"And I could bring dessert. Lemon meringue pie?"

His eyes widened with the true, heartfelt appreciation of someone who'd eaten far too many meals at the local diner. "*Homemade* pie?"

She grinned, suddenly feeling as giddy as a young girl. "Absolutely."

"Then it's a date!"

All the way home she hummed "Some Enchanted Evening," and tapped out the slow, romantic rhythm with her thumbs on the steering wheel.

He'd been joking, of course. It wasn't really a date. But this would be the evening she'd dreamed of in high school—fifty years ago—and she was going to savor every last minute.

For just one evening, she could pretend that she was part of Dan Travers's life.

"COOL," ROSS SAID, studying Grace's outfit as she turned slowly in front of him.

"Really?" She bit her lower lip and stopped to stare at herself in the full-length mirror on the back of her door.

The pile of clothes on her bed bore testament to the impossibility of trying to conceal two-hundred-twenty pounds in anything flattering.

Now in black slacks, a peach overblouse and a loose-fitting, slinky-knit black jacket, she could at least hope to blend into the shadows.

"Tell me this makes me look younger, thinner and taller."

"You look hot." Ross grinned. "And I'm not just saying that because you baked an extra pie for me."

She ruffled his hair. "This isn't a date. I'm just going over to show him how to make some of his favorite dishes."

"Right." Ross glanced pointedly at the discarded outfits on the bed. "I can tell."

"And I won't be late—probably nine, at the very latest. Cook, eat, do dishes, come home."

"Midnight is okay, you know. Remember that when I turn sixteen and can drive."

But would he still be here then? The thought of him leaving always made her feel melancholy. He'd turned into good company, now that his belligerence had softened, and heaven knew he was better off here. But Ashley hadn't called for weeks, and what she planned was anybody's guess.

"I'll remember," Grace promised. "That was a nine o'clock curfew, and not one minute past. And speaking of time, I need to leave. Your supper is in the oven, and if you have any problems, you know my cell phone number."

He rolled his eyes. "I'm fifteen, not five, Aunt Grace. I can handle myself."

It was nervousness, not doubt about Ross that had made her cluck over him like a worried hen as she walked out the door. *I never should have agreed to this supper. What was I thinking? What on earth will I talk about, all that time?* Surely her nervousness would betray her feelings, and she could only imagine how Dan would react if he knew. Tactful kindness, a touch of pity.

He was a very nice man, but that was all too mortifying to even contemplate.

She pulled up in his driveway and resisted the temptation to check her lipstick in the rearview in case he happened to glimpse her from the windows.

And he must have been watching for her, because he came out to her car and opened her door before she even pulled the key out of the ignition.

"I brought your pie," she said as she got out from behind the wheel. "It's in the trunk."

She expected friendliness. A benevolent smile. But there was something quite different in his expression when his gaze swept her from head to toe.

Interest.

"You look lovely tonight," he said. A faint flush appeared on his high cheekbones. "And I need to apologize. I'm just so rusty at all of this. I should have come to get you, and I wasn't even thinking. Forgive me?"

Her old heart gave an extra little flutter as she tentatively rested her hand on his arm. "I'm pretty rusty myself."

Who would have ever thought? She retrieved the pie and followed him into his house…and felt as if a new chapter in her life just might be beginning.

CHAPTER FOURTEEN

GRANT RAN INTO Alex Walthan at the grocery store twice during the next week.

Each time, he'd given the guy a steely glare, but Alex had just stared right back, with all the macho arrogance of a guy in his early twenties who thought he owned the world.

He'd shown none of the body language of someone trying to hide something.

Maybe he was still angry about being dropped from his grandfather's will, but Grant now figured odds were fifty to one the guy hadn't delivered those threats.

And just this morning, Vance Young had stopped in for a brief appointment—dressed as always in his gas station uniform and smelling of pungent motor oil. He was still after an angle to get his child support reduced or eliminated, but Grant had grilled him until the guy had stammered to a confused silence and then capitulated.

After thirty seconds Grant was ninety-percent sure

it hadn't been Vance's voice making those threats on the phone, but grinding the bastard down until he accepted his parental responsibility—at least for that moment—had provided its own satisfaction.

Which left a few other clients and God knew how many other people in the county who might have been involved with or affected by the Blackberry Hill law practice.

The thought made Grant's jaw ache.

And now, he had to look forward to the imminent arrival of Natalie Zimmerman, who'd tearfully called him this morning, needing to see him as soon as possible. He could only hope she was coming on business, and not another, more personal invitation.

She flew in the door a few minutes after one o'clock, her long auburn hair tangled by the wind, her face reddened by the cold. With a quick glance around the empty waiting area, she stormed up to him and grabbed his hand. "Please, we need to talk."

He stepped aside, and she hurried to his office.

"What's up?" he asked as he sauntered down the hall after her.

She was already seated when he walked behind his desk and sat down.

"I'm afraid. Really, truly afraid." Whether the tears in her eyes were from the cold or true emotion he couldn't guess.

"You'll have to be more clear than that. If this is

a police matter…" He rested his fingers on the receiver of the phone, but she shook her head.

"No, not yet." She took a shaky breath. "I think Ray is back in town. I'm almost sure."

"I thought he was in Florida."

"He was—or is. I don't know. But one of my friends thinks she saw him. From a distance."

"At a distance. This time of year, people are dressed in heavy coats. Hats. Gloves. Could be hard to tell from a distance." Grant leaned back in his chair and played with a pencil, though the hairs prickled at the back of his neck. "How sure is she?"

"She knows him well," Natalie said bitterly. "I went to her place often enough when he was drinking."

"When did she think she saw him?"

"She *saw* him two days ago." Natalie's eyes flashed fire. "And I want to know what you can do about it."

"We've still got a restraining order. But that's just to keep him away from you. We can't keep him out of the county."

"But what if he ignores it—comes after me anyway?"

There was the kicker. If Ray chose to go after her, he could do it. He had to know that he'd be a prime suspect, but he could do anything if he was crazy enough and didn't care about the risk of being caught.

"If he violates that order, we can have him arrested. His probation would be revoked and he'd serve his full sentence for his previous offenses if he got in trouble again. Just leaving Florida and not reporting to his officer would do it."

"Not much help to me if I'm dead." She grabbed a tissue out of her handbag and blew her nose.

"If he's in the area, where would he stay?"

"He's got brothers in Three Rivers and Lac du Flambeau. A sister in Green Bay." She blew her nose again. "None of them liked me much, so I can hardly call and ask them."

"I'll ask the sheriff to check them out. Do you feel safe at home?"

Her eyes blazed against her pale face. "Are you kidding? He kicked the door in once when I tried to lock him out. Another time, he threw a barrel through a plate glass window. When he's drinking and mad, there's no telling what he'll do."

"Can you stay with a friend?"

"Right. So he can follow me and put them in danger, too? My friends all have kids. I can't take that risk."

"How about leaving town? Visit some relatives for a while?"

"I got a business to take care of. I can't run like a scared rabbit if Ray decides to show up. But really, I got nowhere to stay. He knows every place I could go."

Grant drummed his fingers on the desk. "Let me call the sheriff and have him check on this. If Ray has been released and is in the area, we'll figure out a safe spot for you. Deal?"

"*Thank* you." She jotted down the names of Ray's siblings and left the paper on Grant's desk, then stood and reached across the desk to grasp one of his hands. "I'll be waiting."

After she walked out the door, Grant called the sheriff's office and left a message for him, then began gathering files for a four o'clock deposition in Kendrick and a dinner meeting there at five-thirty.

It certainly was possible that Ray was free. With the help of a sharp lawyer, bad guys got back on the streets almost faster than the paperwork could be done.

And if he'd been released, Natalie had good reason to be afraid...and yet another possibility existed. Could Ray have been the caller?

AT SIX O'CLOCK, Grant pulled to the side of the road, shifted his new cell phone to his other ear and grabbed a steno pad from the glove box of his car. "You talked to who?"

"The Walthan kid, yesterday." The sheriff paused, apparently studying his notes. "He has an attitude, but I think I got through to him. Being on a short list of suspects oughta deter anyone who isn't stupid."

"And Vance Young?"

"Ah, the guy who's livid about child support. He's

still convinced you're incompetent for not getting him out of paying what he owes." Randy snorted in derision. "I'm turning his name over to the county for special attention regarding his overdue payment, and he knows it. I think he'll be lying low for a while."

"What about Ray Zimmerman?"

"Florida, far as we know. He was released…" Randy paused. "Let's see—here it is, February 15."

Grant cursed under his breath. "After only four months?"

"Lawyer got him out on a technicality."

"But he's on probation, surely."

"Checks in once a month. Has a job…at a welding shop, and he's current on his rent. He oughta be out of the picture."

"You're *sure* he's still down there?"

"His boss told the probation officer he works forty to fifty hours a week, but I've contacted the other county sheriffs up here so they can check in on his siblings." Randy cleared his throat. "The other names you gave me didn't pan out—no local addresses and no one has seen them around."

"So we've hit a dead end?"

"Maybe. I'll keep sending a patrol car up to Jill's place at night to check on her. You let me know if you hear anything more, okay? The guy harassing you is going to slip up one of these times, and then we'll get him."

Grant disconnected the call and stared at the road ahead. Maybe their troubles were over, though.

With Ray still down in Florida, Natalie should feel safer, and the anonymous caller hadn't made a move in two weeks. Perhaps he was one of the suspects the sheriff had already questioned…and had gotten cold feet about his little vendetta.

Grant shifted back into drive and got back on the highway, but one word kept playing through his thoughts.

Retribution.

Would someone angry enough to promise retribution be so easily scared away?

"I'M HEADING OUT," Donna called from the back door of the clinic. "See you tomorrow morning after your breakfast."

"Right." But Jill could barely imagine joining the other doctors and Erin Reynolds for their weekly breakfast meeting at Ollie's Diner.

Chatting normally, acting as if nothing earth-shaking had happened to her eight hours earlier was beyond her.

Just thinking about the rich, cloying aromas of the café's renowned cinnamon rolls and trucker-sized breakfasts made her stomach lurch.

The three other docs would take one look at her reaction and give her the diagnosis she'd received from that plastic strip this morning.

Pregnant.

She couldn't remember the number of times she'd confirmed that news to patients. Most had been overjoyed. Some terrified, some angry. Some stunned and bewildered. And now she could relate to every one of those women, because each of those emotions had been thundering through her all day. *Pregnant. Pregnant. Pregnant.*

And there wasn't one thing she could—or would—do to change that fact, no matter what.

Bracing her palms on the desk, she bowed her head, overwhelmed by how this was going to change her life. Her career. And, regrettably, the opinions of a lot of people in town. It was quite a joke that the doctor herself had been so careless.

Except she hadn't, not really.

She'd had protected sex with a man who was still her husband—even if they were on the brink of divorce. She'd made *sure* they'd been careful.

And the irony of it all was that pregnancy had been one of the bigger issues in their marriage. Because her one driving force in life had been that she would never follow in the footsteps of her mother.

With a bitter laugh, she raised her eyes to the small, gilt-framed photograph on the bookshelf next to her desk.

It wasn't a studio photo—there'd never been enough money for that. It was a candid shot of a careworn woman who'd soon die of emphysema because she couldn't pay for medical care.

Next to her stood four young children—the legacy of a drunk who'd fathered the first two, and a drifter who'd stayed around long enough to father two more before taking off.

The woman in the picture had made choices that left her exhausted and overwhelmed, and her children without a father.

"Well, Mom, I'm following in your footsteps," Jill whispered to the empty room. "I guess I'm not so different after all."

CHAPTER FIFTEEN

BLINDING SUNSHINE REFLECTED off the snowbanks along the main street of downtown Blackberry Hill.

Grace squinted as she stepped out of her car and made her way down the unevenly shoveled sidewalk, wishing she'd thought to bring her clip-on sunglasses this morning.

So far, she'd filled her blood pressure and diabetes meds at the pharmacy, dropped off the rental DVDs Ross had watched last night and had been to Frannie's Beauty Salon for a luxury she rarely allowed herself—a wash and set.

She caught a reflection of herself in the hardware store window and her spirits sagged. A hairstylist couldn't salvage a sixty-something face that had seen too many years. A few new outfits couldn't conceal the short, squat body of a Swedish troll.

And she was just kidding herself, thinking that a man like Dan Travers really wanted to see her again.

Still, they'd laughed and talked until midnight last

Saturday—reminiscing about their high school days and sharing fond memories of Leah.

And maybe that was all it was. A moment in time for both of them to remember being young, and for him to feel in touch with his beloved wife once again.

Yet when he'd walked Grace outside that night, he'd lingered at her car, one hand on the top of the open door, and he'd asked if he could treat *her* the next time. At Dawson's, the fancy supper club out on Lake William.

She'd been there for hospital board dinner meetings, but never on a *date*. She worried at her lower lip. No one dressed up in long dresses and sequins at a place like that—or anywhere in the county, for that matter, except maybe at Christmas— but she'd seen women of the country club set there, decked out in little black dresses and sparkly earrings.

As if.

She kept walking, past the bank and Ollie's Diner, then slowed as she approached Lindsey's Lost Treasures, an upscale consignment shop one of her former nurses had opened last year.

Self-conscious, she glanced up and down the street, then stepped inside. The fragrance of potpourri filled the air, and the soft light of candles flickered on the old-fashioned, glass-fronted display case just inside the door.

Lindsey herself swept toward her, with a broad smile and outstretched hands. She gave Grace a small hug. "It's wonderful to see you again! I haven't been back up to the hospital in *ages*."

"I still wish I had ten of you. If you ever want to pick up some hours, just let me know."

"I sometimes wish I had ten of me, too, just to keep up with this." Lindsey chuckled and waved a hand toward the back of the store. "Have you been here lately? I've added an infant and children's section in back, along with maternity wear. If my business loan goes through I plan to expand into the empty shop next door and add a furniture area."

"You're doing well." Grace smiled back at her, but she already wished she hadn't stopped.

Flirty little beaded dresses hung from their spaghetti straps on a rack near the front. Displayed on the wall were several tiny, glittery tops…all about the size to fit a ten-year-old girl, from what Grace could tell. And Lindsey herself looked as if she'd blow away on a stiff breeze.

The younger woman's delicate eyebrows drew together. "Is there anything I can help you with? Clothes? Gift items?"

"No…I was just out walking…" A pretty pin in the display case caught her eye. Twinkling in a rainbow of colors, it had been fashioned into the shape of a peacock.

Lindsey followed her gaze, and then cocked her head and studied Grace from head to toe. "Beautiful piece, isn't it? And we have the prettiest outfit—a perfect way to show it off. I'll bet it'd fit you just right."

"Well…" Grace wavered.

"Just came in yesterday. The consigner brings in lovely items, and most of them have barely been worn. This outfit still has its store tags." Lindsey flashed a grin. "I'll even give you twenty percent off, since this is your first time here."

Trapped by the younger woman's enthusiasm, Grace followed her to the middle of the store, where the racks were marked as women's sizes.

In deep azure-blue, the loose-fitting jacket sparkled and swirled as Lindsey lifted the hanger from the rack with a flourish. "It has just a dusting of glitter for evening," she explained. "But you could still find a lot of places to wear it. With the long, straight-cut dress underneath, it has a very slender silhouette." She held out the hanger. "Want to try?"

It was beautiful. She'd never had anything like it. Would she look silly, dressing up too much for what was just a simple thank-you dinner?

Lindsey pursed her lips. "It sets off your pretty silver hair and those blue, blue eyes of yours, too. But please, don't let me railroad you into trying it on." Her dimples deepened. "My husband says I'm the pushiest person on the planet, and he should know!"

"Show me to the dressing room. If I don't at least try it, I know I'm going to be sorry."

Grace took the hanger and followed Lindsey's directions to the back of the store, past the shoe display and children's wear.

A lone shopper stood near the newborn outfits, her head bowed. Her glossy brown hair, swept up in a casual twist, and the back of her leather jacket looked so familiar....

Grace faltered mid-stride, self-conscious over the glamorous dress draped over her arm. "Jill?"

Jill stiffened and turned abruptly, gripping a packaged layette set too tightly, a wary look in her wide brown eyes. "Hi, Grace. I was just looking. For my...cousin."

How odd. "That's nice."

Jill's gaze flicked nervously to the dress Grace held. "Pretty."

They stared at each other for a moment, then they both broke into helpless laughter.

"I'm an old fool, thinking I can play dress-up and lose thirty years and fifty pounds in the process."

"And I—" Jill's smile faded as she lowered her voice. The plastic packaging of the layette set crackled beneath her trembling fingers. "I just lied. I'm in a position I never thought I'd be in. Especially not now, and I can't imagine how I'm going to handle it."

Jill was in her early thirties. A professional woman. But right now Grace wished she could give her friend a big, smothering hug, and try to make things better.

"Let me try this dress on, and tell me what you think. Then we ought to go over to Ollie's for a talk. Deal?"

THE BACK BOOTH at Ollie's was filled with an early lunch crowd, so they ended up in the next booth at the far end. With the high wooden booth dividers and the hubbub of the busy diner, they'd still have privacy.

Jill tensed as she slid into her seat, waiting for her stomach to get queasy, but the morning aromas of bacon, sausage and heavy caramel rolls had dissipated. *Thank goodness.*

"I'm just stunned," Jill said in a low voice, leaning over the table between them with her hands twisted in a tight knot. She forced her hands to relax. "It was the night Patsy passed away. I was already upset, then that guy drove up behind my car and rammed my bumper. Grant came along, and…"

"Totally understandable. And what's to explain? You're still married, after all."

Grace's grandmotherly smile settled some of the butterflies in Jill's stomach, though the enormity of the situation still felt like a vise pressing down on her chest. "With the way gossip spreads in a small town, I'm essentially divorced already. And the fact that I've given birth-control lectures to every teen in the county by now, this is going to ruin my credibility with them *and* it's going to be laughable to everyone else."

"Honey, it's nobody's business…for all they

know, you've gotten back together." Grace reached across the table and patted her hand. "The gossip can fly about *that*."

"I suppose." Jill shook her head slowly. "The biggest dilemma is how to tell Grant. And with the way things stand between us now, I can't imagine what he'll say."

Grace idly stirred another packet of sweetener into her coffee. "Maybe he'll surprise you."

"It'll be no surprise—he'll be stunned. Angry. He wanted kids more than anything in the world. I did, too, but much later…our priorities were just never the same on anything that mattered. Now this—" She managed a laugh that sounded bitter even to her ears. "This will be like a slap in the face."

"But he'll still have to be excited about being a father, even if you two aren't together."

Jill stared at the untouched glass of orange juice in front of her. "Once he calms down and thinks about it. Though I'm sure he'd much rather have had this news with a new wife, not the old one."

Grace's head bobbed up. "Is he seeing someone *already?*"

"I wouldn't know. I don't think so." She thought about the condo he'd purchased in Kendrick and the trips he made there, sometimes overnight. "Maybe."

Grace frowned. "There was that woman last fall. Red hair."

"Natalie. I heard all the rumors then, too, and I've recently seen them together at his office, but I don't think he had an affair back then. Now? His time is his own, I guess."

"Not until he's actually *divorced*."

Her staunch support reminded Jill of Donna back at the clinic. Yet another person she was going to have to tell about her...situation. "It's going to be pretty embarrassing if he thinks this pregnancy was an intentional ploy to get him back. He probably already thinks I'm pathetic and needy, after I was so upset that night."

"Takes two to tango, in case he doesn't realize it, and we both know the failure stats on birth control." Grace bristled. "And what woman—*or man*—wouldn't be emotional over poor Patsy's death?"

"That's my view," Jill said dryly. "I'm just hoping that he sees it that way...and not as some nefarious plot intended to snare him. Because believe me, I don't want him back."

Grace's mouth pursed, as if she didn't quite believe it. "What about you? That's the important thing. Are you excited about the baby? Or is it just too overwhelming right now?"

"Excited. Confused. A little scared in the face of a lifetime commitment. I know it will work out. I love the babies I see at the clinic, and I've always known I wanted a family someday. I just figured I would be happily married when it happened." But now, after finally talking about it with someone, she did feel reassured. "So, tell me about that beautiful dress you just bought. You looked fantastic, by the way."

Grace colored. "I'm just a silly old woman, I guess."

"Aah. Dan Travers. And by the way, you aren't that old."

"Ross urged me to 'go for it,' and I guess I did. I ran into Dan in the grocery, and we talked…then I went over to his place and helped him make a dinner." She shrugged. "He's just reciprocating with dinner out at Dawson's Sunday evening. That's all."

"Maybe not, with that dress," Jill said, smiling. "You looked pretty hot."

"He'll probably just want to talk about the old days again, and his wife. I wouldn't have thought it, with his busy career, but I got the feeling he's lonely."

"No matter how hectic the days are, nights can still be long." Jill glanced at her watch, then reached into her purse for her billfold. She dropped a five-dollar bill on the table.

Grace reached for her purse, too, but Jill shook her head. "I've got it."

"Thanks. I'm glad we had a chance to talk."

Jill grinned. "We'll have to meet again next week and report back on how things went."

"I'll wish us both luck," Grace muttered. "And next time, the coffee's on me."

Someone brushed past Jill, bumping her as she slid out of the booth. "Sorry," she called after him.

He lifted a dismissive hand and kept walking, his head down. The hair at the back of her neck prickled.

She watched him leave, hoping for a glimpse of his face, but he didn't turn. "Did you see who that was?"

Grace gave her a curious look. "No…the bill of his cap was too low. I really wasn't paying any attention, anyway. Why?"

A waitress wound her way through the tables and stopped at the booth. "All done, ladies?"

"Thanks, yes." Jill focused on her name tag. "By the way, Kristie, do you happen to know the guy who just left? Black ball cap, jean jacket?"

"Never seen him before, but I'm sorta new in town."

"Did he pay by credit card?"

The waitress pursed her lips and leaned back to glance at the last booth. "Cash." She gave Grace a worried frown. "Is he a bad debt or something?"

"No…I was just curious about his name. I know I've seen him somewhere…." Jill thought for a second, then added in a conspiratorial whisper, "And I was sure he was someone famous. If he comes in again, you should ask. I'd love to know!"

GRACE BUSTLED TO her car, her new dress slung over her arm in a full-length, translucent pink plastic bag.

Misgivings mingled with anticipation as she

unlocked her car door and hung the dress on a hook inside. A new dress, a foolish old woman. *What* had she been thinking when she'd agreed to this—this *date* tomorrow evening?

Lost in thought, she jerked back at the sound of her name to see Warren standing on the sidewalk.

"Looks like you're getting all dolled up," he observed. "Big date?"

"Dinner. Out on Lake William."

He studied her closely for moment, then threw back his head and laughed. "No, this is a big, *big* date, I think. You're blushing, Gracey."

"It's the cold, Warren. I don't blush."

"Ha!" He stepped off the curb and joined her at her car door. "But you do look a little…edgy. What gives?"

"I thought you were leaving for Florida right after you got out of the hospital."

"Changed my mind." He grinned. "New dress. Snazzy hair. Who's the lucky guy?"

She couldn't quite meet his gaze. "Dan."

"Well, well. It's about time."

Uncomfortable with the knowing look in his eyes, Grace hitched a shoulder and tried for nonchalance. "It doesn't mean anything. I…probably shouldn't have agreed."

"Hey, Travers, a good dinner, moonlight over the lake, and you have second thoughts? Dance the night away!"

She fingered her keys, wanting nothing more than to climb into her car and drive away, but not quite able to escape the kindness in his voice.

"What's the matter?" He cocked his head, thinking. "You don't like him after all?"

"Of course, but…"

"You've had a better offer that same night."

"Of course not."

"You hate Dawson's?"

"It's lovely."

"And you will be, too. Never doubt that, Gracey." His expression softened. "I know it feels strange, dating at our age. Awkward. Maybe a little silly. But we deserve companionship as much as all those twenty-somethings."

"What about you, then?"

"Someday." He gave her a lopsided smile. "In time."

But she doubted that was true. Outside of their careers, he and his wife had rarely been seen without each other. They'd held hands walking down the street and had called each other "honey" and "sweetie," even in public. She couldn't remember ever hearing them call each other by their given names. What was it like, sharing a love like that?

"I'd…better be going," Grace said, her heart suddenly heavy.

She was behind the wheel and pulling her door shut when Warren called her name.

"Dancing," he said. "You're worried about the dancing!"

"O-of course not," she sputtered.

"That's it, isn't it?"

She might not have admitted it to anyone else, but Warren was one of her oldest friends. "Maybe. I'd look like an old fool if I even tried."

For all that he liked to tease, Warren surprised her by simply nodding thoughtfully. "That could be a problem. A dark, romantic restaurant. Candles flickering. Music. The perfect night—until you insist on sitting out every dance."

"I'm sure it won't be a big deal. In fact, I'll bet Dan doesn't dance, either."

"Dance with me, Gracey."

"What?"

"Not here. My place or yours, for maybe a half hour or so, and then you'll have the basic steps down. Of course, it's up to you." He shrugged. "Me? I'd want to enjoy every minute if I had a date with someone really special."

Embarrassment flooded through her...coupled with gratitude for his friendship and tact. "Deal. If I can pay you back with a pie."

"Lemon meringue?"

"And a raisin cream."

MONDAY MORNINGS AT the clinic were always hectic. This one had proved even more so than most, with the scheduled patients plus a surge of calls about adult influenza symptoms, probable ear infections in the under-three-year-old set and two ankle sprains related to the icy sidewalks in town.

And, sitting in front of her right now, yet another ice fishing calamity.

More often than not she saw frostbite and various body parts impaled by fishhooks. This hardy old gent had a nasty auger laceration from his weekend fishing expedition, but had refused to leave his little icehouse and risk missing the chance to catch a big one.

His annoyed daughter had come right into the exam room with him and now stood with her arms folded over her very pregnant belly, glaring at him as Jill thoroughly cleaned his arm.

Already, there was considerable heat—and in-flammation—edging the wound. "You should have gone to the E.R.," Jill said. "It's too late to suture this, and you're going to have a bigger scar."

He snorted. "Not like that matters. Hell, I'm eighty-two. No one's gonna look to see if these arms are pretty."

"This also shows signs of infection, Sam. Given your heart disease and diabetes, that's not good." She reached for the tray Donna had set on the counter and lightly wrapped the arm. "The nurse will be here in a minute with a tetanus booster, and I'm writing you a prescription for antibiotics. Ten days. Can you follow through on that?"

"He will," his daughter announced. "He lives with me, and I'll make sure of it."

"When you have that baby, you can stop mothering me." He scowled at her, but there was affection in his eyes as well. "Took her and her hubby fifteen years, but it finally happened."

"Congratulations." The woman had to be close to forty, if not a shade older…and certainly in the high-risk category. A casual glance at her feet revealed painfully swollen ankles. "When are you due?"

"Beginning of May, Dr. Reynolds says." The woman's tense expression eased, her smile lighting her face. "We don't exactly know the dates. After years of trying, this was a very big surprise."

Jill finished up and paged Donna on the intercom, then moved on to the next exam room where Zachary Farrell awaited his four-month well-child physical.

His young, harried mother had corralled her two active toddlers in the room and held the baby in her arms.

"Shut the door," Eve urged, grabbing for one of the toddler's arms to keep him from racing out. She laughed, but there was a hint of desperation in her voice. "If they get loose, we'll never catch 'em. They *know* why we come to this place."

Jill closed the door and crouched at eye level with the two-year-olds. They were twins, well-dressed, and identical down to the cowlicks on the tops of their heads. Each had juice stains down the front of his pale blue sweatshirt.

She smiled and offered them colorful stickers. "Hi, guys. We're just looking at your little brother today. Is that okay?"

One of them darted behind his mother's legs. The other popped a thumb in his mouth and shyly accepted the present before backing away, his eyes wide and wary.

"That's pretty good," their mother chuckled. "Last time, we had to fish them out from behind the exam table."

"They're adorable. I always thought that if I ever had children, I'd love twins."

The mother's mouth dropped open. "You're kidding. Of course, you're a professional. You could probably handle septuplets and never blink an eye."

"Hardly. I truly admire moms who do a great job day after day. *Especially* when they're dealing with toddlers and babies at the same time." Jill winked at the little boy in front of her, then straightened and moved to the small desk in the corner. She opened the baby's medical file. "I see his weight, height and head circumference are fine. Is he sleeping well for you?"

Eve brought the baby over to the exam table and chattered about his routine as Jill began the physical. The toddlers clambered at Eve's knees until she hoisted them both onto a chair so they could watch—though she held each securely by his overall straps.

When Jill finished her exam and Donna came in with the syringes for the baby's vaccinations, Eve settled the boys on the floor. "How is he?"

"Zachary is doing great. Everything is normal and he's right on the mark for growth," Jill said as she filled out the billing slip and handed it over. "Do you have any questions?"

Eve blew at her bangs. "Just tell me where I can find a few more hours every day."

Although she'd ended up in family medicine, Jill had done a residency in pediatrics. She'd provided medical care for hundreds—perhaps thousands—of children then, during her first job in Chicago, and now here. She knew the medical side of caring for children, but watching the offhand, easy competence of this woman suddenly made her realize just how little she knew about hands-on parenting.

And how challenging life would be in the very near future.

"How do you manage?" Jill asked. "Really—the constant supervision, the responsibility. Day after day."

Eve raised her brows in surprise. "You just love them," she said simply. "You treasure every day. At least, you do at night, when you've survived the day and they're in their clean jammies, sleeping like angels. Some days are a *bit* of a challenge."

"I'll bet they are." Jill grinned down at the boys, who were now struggling into their winter coats and obviously eager to escape before they ended up on the exam table, too. "You're doing a great job with these little guys."

Eve chuckled. "Starting off with twins was a trial by fire. I used to think my house had to be perfect. Now, I figure a little dirt never hurt anyone, and if the house is a wreck, so be it. What's more important than spending time with the kids?"

Long after the last patient left for the day, Jill thought about the middle-aged woman joyously facing her high-risk pregnancy, and the deep contentment in Eve's eyes when she'd talked about priorities. And how Patsy's last worries had been about her children.

There would be difficulties ahead. Single parenting was never easy, but it would all work out. This pregnancy could be the start of the most rewarding, wonderful step in her life.

But at this early stage nothing was certain. She'd counseled all too many distraught couples on the fact that a good fifteen percent of pregnancies ended in an early miscarriage—sometimes before the woman was even sure she was pregnant—through no fault of her own.

So she would wait awhile, and make absolutely

sure before she told Grant. A few more weeks, maybe. A month.

Whatever his reaction, there was no way she'd even consider ending her pregnancy. But perhaps it would be kinder and—she had to admit—easier to simply postpone sharing the news. What harm could there be?

CHAPTER SIXTEEN

"HEY, ROSS! I saw your grandma at the supper club with Principal Travers," Josh hooted across the Resource Room. "They looked *real* cozy."

Ross slid down in his chair and ignored him, but he felt heat moving up his neck.

Mrs. French looked up from the paper on Brooke's desk and frowned. "This is study time, Josh. *Quiet.*"

Never one to sit still or keep his thoughts to himself, Josh bounded out of his chair and came to stand at Ross's desk. "But I did see them. We went out there for my dad's birthday on Saturday night. Wow, you oughta do good in school if your grandma hangs with the principal!"

"She's my great-*aunt,*" Ross said automatically, feeling the eyes of the entire class on him. "They were friends back in high school."

"Friends? I saw them hold hands!"

Josh was practically trembling with excitement

over his revelation to the class, and Ross imagined the satisfaction of shoving him over the next row of desks. "They're *old*," he ground out, glaring at Josh. "Maybe he was helping her, or something." Out of the corner of his eye he saw Mrs. French take a step in their direction. "Anyway, what's it to you?"

Josh's glee faded and he looked away, as if he'd finally realized his mistake. "I...dunno. It was...cool, I guess."

"It's cool. *Now go sit down.*"

Clearly deflated, Josh turned away, and the teacher went back to helping Brooke. Ross felt a light tap on his shoulder.

"He can be such a jerk," Mandy whispered. "But he doesn't mean it. Maybe he forgot his Ritalin."

Ross shrugged and bent over his homework without looking back at her. "I guess."

Mandy had lost her school driving permit over their accident back in February. She'd walked with him to and from school a couple times...until her dad drove past them one day and ordered her to get in his car, *now.*

As her car door closed Ross had heard the words *"inner-city punk"* and *"no good."*

The memory still had the power to make him cringe. The next day, Mandy had apologized, but he still gave her wide berth in the hallways and tried to keep his distance in the classes they shared.

Maybe he'd been in a little trouble back in Chicago, but he'd kept to himself here and was probably going to pull a 3.5 GPA this term. "No good punk" hadn't fit him before, and it sure didn't now.

His old anger bubbled up inside him as he went to the rest of his Tuesday morning classes, his head down. The temptation to skip out at lunchtime brought him to the back door of the school near the cafeteria, where steps led down the side of a loading dock. He could've easily slipped away.

Except that Grace would find out, and she'd be disappointed.

And Travers had not only taken Grace out Saturday night, but he'd come over for Sunday dinner and Grace had been humming to herself ever since. If that wasn't awkward enough—having your principal eating roast beef and apple pie across the table from you—surely it would be ten times worse if Ross did anything stupid.

With a heavy sigh, he turned away.

The sound of faint, male voices outside the door sounded vaguely familiar, but he just kept walking—until one voice rose above the rest. Angry, but tinged with fear. *Mandy.*

He pulled to a halt. Listened. Then spun on his heel and hurried out the set of double doors.

Hemmed in by walls on two sides and a five-foot drop off the dock on the other, Mandy stood shivering in the cold, clutching her notebook to her chest, her face pale.

Ted and Boyd faced her. Boyd snickered, and moved closer. "I still think you owe me, bitch."

Mandy looked at Ross, then back to the other boys. "I don't owe you a *thing*."

"Yeah? Well, I think you do." The two crowded in closer. Ted shoved her shoulder. "You think you're special, 'cause your daddy's rich. But we know different."

Ross dropped his backpack to the dock and swallowed hard. "Leave her alone."

Startled, both boys spun around guiltily. Then Ted's face twisted into a sneer and he elbowed his friend. "*Big* threat. Hey, I think he needs to learn a lesson."

"Mandy, come on over here," Ross said quietly. He stared baldly at them, and hoped he was a convincing liar. "Coach Miller's on his way."

But Boyd thrust out a beefy arm so she couldn't pass. "I doubt it, jerk. He doesn't ever stay here over lunch."

"He did today."

Ted wavered, but Boyd swore, lowered his head and charged as if he was back on the football field.

Both guys had reputations as powerful fullbacks. But neither of them had grown up in a tough area of Chicago.

Ross stepped aside at the last second and caught him

in the jaw with his fist, then kneed him at the back of the legs as he passed, a victim of his own momentum.

Boyd stumbled. Wavered at the edge of the dock, then fell sideways down the steps with a howl of pain.

Ross turned to Ted and glared at him. "How about you? Or maybe you just like taking on little girls half your size? You are *pathetic*."

Ted took a step forward, then his gaze veered to his friend, who'd curled up in a ball clutching his arm. He stood there like a big, dumb ox, his face a mask of uncertainty. Then his expression changed to one of innocence as he looked over Ross's shoulder.

"Mr. Travers! I'm glad you got here. This kid just attacked us, and I think he broke Boyd's arm."

Already hidden in the shadows, Mandy disappeared when Travers and a clutch of students crowded out onto the loading dock. Someone sent for the school nurse and soon she was outside, prodding at Boyd's arm, then wrapping it in a sling.

She led him away with a comforting, supporting hand on his good arm and, as she opened the back door and let Boyd through, she gave Ross a withering stare.

Travers ordered the rest of the students inside. "Ross, Ted—I want you two in my office. Now."

Like a calf going to slaughter, Ross followed Ted and the principal down the hall. At the door of the office, Ted smirked at him. He and Boyd would hardly have trouble coordinating their stories. They'd just say he'd started it and landed the first punch.

And Mandy, whose father was so temperamental, wouldn't dare say a word.

Ross paced the tiny waiting area of Travers's office. Sweat trickled down his back and he could feel the heavy thud of his heartbeat counting off the seconds, the minutes. They'd been waiting more than a half hour and still Travers hadn't come out to get either one of them.

Ted lounged insolently in one of the chairs, his smirk still in place. "Bad news, you hurting one of the school's big football stars. In case you haven't heard, this school has a no tolerance policy. It expels kids like you for fighting."

"Some *stars*," Ross shot back under his breath, "if you get your kicks out of harassing girls."

But though he glared at the other boy, the enormity of Ted's words twisted through his gut like a knife. *Expelled.*

There was no other high school in this town. No other option. He'd be back in Chicago, having to deal with Tony every day. Trapped. And though he'd been angry about being dumped here, it was the best thing that could have happened to him, and he didn't want it to end.

Travers finally appeared at his office door and called Ted's name. Five minutes later, the boy came out of the office with a cocky grin. "See you around, loser."

But he didn't leave the waiting area. He slumped into a seat across the room with an expression of boredom. Travers called Ross's name a moment later.

Inside the man's office, Ross dropped into his usual seat and rested his forearms on his thighs. It had been bad coming here before. But now—with Travers spending time with Aunt Grace—it was far worse.

Travers watched him for a moment, his eyebrows drawn together. "I thought you should know that Boyd is all right. No broken bones, just some bruising to his arm and his pride."

Ross swallowed hard. "Good."

"But we still do not condone physical violence of any kind in this school. If there's trouble, a student should back away. Find a peaceful solution. If necessary, he should find a teacher to handle the situation. As much as I hate to—"

The intercom on his desk beeped. He pressed a button and leaned close to listen, then murmured something back. A moment later Mandy walked in, her cheeks pink and her father close behind.

The glower on Welbourne's face made Ross wish the floor would open and swallow him up.

"Mandy has something to say, Travers."

Welbourne crossed his arms across his chest and

stood in the doorway like an armed guard, and Ross was suddenly very glad he didn't have a father like *him*.

She darted a quick, apologetic glance at Ross, then fixed her gaze on the edge of Travers's desk. "I…um…went outside during lunch. I wasn't feeling so good and I thought the fresh air would help…but Boyd and Teddy followed me. They were both really piss—uh—angry that I wouldn't let them copy my algebra homework before class. When I…um…laid into them about it, they got even more mad. They started crowding in, and Ted shoved me. And that's when Ross came out. He told them to back off, and Boyd charged him. Boyd started it, not Ross."

Travers pursed his lips. "I didn't see you out there, Mandy."

Her cheeks turned a darker pink. "I took off when everyone else showed up. I was embarrassed, and I knew I'd get in trouble, too." She darted a furtive glance at her father.

"So Boyd and Ted started this."

"Yes, sir." Her lower lip trembled. "I'm really sorry about leaving like that, and letting Ross get in trouble. I called my dad at work and… It just isn't fair, if you expel Ross for something that wasn't his fault."

"I see." Travers swiveled his chair back to face Ross. "What do you have to say about this?"

Ross opened his mouth, then shut it and shifted uneasily in his seat. No one snitched—it was one of the first rules in high school. Yet if he didn't speak up, Mandy might look like a liar. "I…uh…"

"He can't say," Welbourne broke in, his voice gruff. "You know that as well as I do."

Surprised, Ross jerked his gaze to Mandy's father.

"I haven't liked this Ross kid much. But those two punks threatened my daughter and, if he hadn't stepped in, they could have done much worse to her. As it is, I'm ready to press charges against Boyd for assault."

"Daddy!" Mandy's eyes widened in horror as she turned to grab his arm. "Please, no."

Welbourne patted her hand. "And I think this boy here should be commended for doing what's right."

Travers's expression softened. "I appreciate your honesty, Mandy. And I appreciate that your dad took the time to come in with you." He looked at the clock on the wall. "Ross and Mandy, you'd better get to your next classes, and I'll discuss this further with Mr. Welbourne."

A reprieve. Ross stood and headed for the door.

"Thank you, son." Mr. Welbourne thrust a hand forward and Ross awkwardly shook it. "I may be a little protective with my children, but I'm not afraid to admit being wrong."

The bell rang as Ross and Mandy stepped out of the main office. Students surged out of every open doorway down the hallway, the noise and commotion in stark contrast to the quiet of Travers's office.

"Thanks, Mandy," he said as he shouldered one strap of his backpack. "Without you there, I might have been on my way back to Chicago."

"I'm just sorry I didn't stick around in the first place." She worried at her lower lip. "Now I have to make sure Daddy doesn't do anything stupid about those charges. It would be all over school, and everyone would start whispering about me *wanting* to be outside with those guys. I'd be labeled a slut, and when football season came and those guys couldn't play…" She shuddered. "Every time we lost a game, it would be my fault."

If there hadn't been a hallway full of witnesses rushing past, he might have given her a hug. "Those jerks deserve whatever they get." He smiled at her. "Just don't worry. I'm sure the principal will do the right thing."

"I hope so."

And then, despite all the students jostling past them, she smiled, stretched up to brush a kiss against his cheek, and then she melted into the crowd.

GRANT GLANCED AT the caller ID on his desk phone and smiled. Picking up the receiver, he tipped back his chair, already aware that this would be a long call.

It had been a damned strange week. Dad had stayed in town after his discharge from the hospital, despite his earlier plans to head straight to Florida.

Then suddenly—bright and early Monday morning—he'd mumbled something about needing to get away. He'd used a discount-airfare site online, put in a low bid and had arranged for a flight south the next afternoon.

Now, as usual, he wasted no time on pleasantries. "So, what's going on today?"

Grant tapped a pencil on the desk as he ticked off the list of appointments scheduled for the day, the two no-shows.

"The Millbrook case?"

He referred to an ongoing battle regarding an easement between a back-to-nature client and Bob Millbrook, a local landowner with visions of a trailer park development. If he could gain better access to the property.

"Over, in our favor. Millbrook claims the whole deal cost him tens of thousands of dollars and he's going to sue, but time will tell."

"And Vance Young?"

"He was back in here yesterday. Steaming. I've told him exactly what you would've told him yourself about his child support, but that man just won't give it up. He's livid about his ex moving on to a new boyfriend."

"He needs to be in therapy."

"No kidding. I envision that guy losing control someday."

Warren continued firing questions about clients until Grant finally called a time-out. "You know, Dad—you're supposed to be on vacation."

"I am. And I'll tell you, it's not what it's cracked up to be."

"You've only been gone a couple days. What about all that nice warm weather?"

"Old folks like sitting around in the sun. Not me."

Grant smothered a laugh, guessing that his father would never consider himself one of the "old folks" even if he lived to a hundred. "When you're feeling a little stronger, maybe you can start playing golf."

"I doubt that will happen," Warren said irritably, "with your Uncle Fred watching me like he thinks I'm going to keel over, and your Aunt Jane hovering like a hen."

"I know it's not the same being there without Mom," Grant said gently. "It can't be. But it's been three years. Maybe you can use this time to find something else to enjoy besides the law."

Warren fell silent.

"Dad?" Grant closed his eyes, wishing he hadn't been so blunt. His parents had been inseparable until the day his mother died, and no one knew better than Grant just how devastating her death had been to the husband she left behind.

"Yeah…look, I'd better get moving. Jane has some sort of tea party at the club, and she's dragging

Fred and me along so we'll bid at the silent auction. It's a benefit of some kind."

"Have a good time, and relax." Grant hesitated, struggling over the words that were so hard to say aloud. "I love you, Dad."

But Warren had already hung up.

AN HOUR LATER, Grant hit the security code of the panel inside his father's house and walked into the kitchen. He tossed his keys and leather gloves on the counter and pulled open the refrigerator door.

No surprise there. A half gallon of milk, the usual condiments and the six-pack of Bud Light Warren must have purchased before his heart attack. Grant had tossed the molding perishables his first night here, and had mostly eaten out ever since.

But that got old, and if he'd thought to stop at the grocery store on the way home he would have thrown together something easy, like cornmeal waffles and cheddar scrambled eggs.

With a sigh, he pulled out the deli ham and Swiss Lorraine cheese he'd bought a couple days ago, and assembled a towering sandwich on rye.

Grabbing one of the beers, he shoved the door shut with his hip and set up at the dining room table. Silence was a good thing, he reminded himself as he hit the light switch for the chandelier. He'd had a typically busy Thursday, and he could get a lot done.

The briefcase he'd dropped by the back door held hours of work that needed to be finished before he made his usual Tuesday run to the Kendrick office next week. Since his phone call this afternoon, Dad had e-mailed twice for advice on some medical and hospital bills that were being forwarded to Florida.

And, come to think of it, Phil had called earlier today to remind him that Sadie was due for her rabies vaccination.

Grant's mood lifted. *That* was certainly important. He'd have to call—or maybe stop by so he could let Jill know.

She'd made it perfectly clear more than three weeks ago that they'd always been wrong for each other. Of course she was right. They'd had no business spending that night together. But at least they were civil, unlike many of the divorce clients he dealt with.

Her philosophy about *friendship* didn't exactly work, though.

They ran into each other almost every day—at the post office, at the grocery store, at the bank. He found himself up at Chapel Hill checking on Sadie, or finding some other excuse to stop in.

But after years of intimacy, it was awkward just being friends. Yet he missed her wit, her laughter and surprising insights. The camaraderie, and the physical side of their relationship as well.

And whenever he saw her, he found it increasingly difficult to imagine never seeing her again.

So when the title problems on the house were finally resolved, he would get around to meeting with *her* lawyer, settle their business affairs, and be done, once and for all. They could go their separate ways.

And by then Grant would be back in Kendrick full time, so it would be a good, clean break.

He went to get his briefcase to do some work while he ate, but saw the blinking light on the answering machine as he passed, and stopped to check the messages.

Four calls for donations to worthy causes.

One alumni association offering a Visa card.

Someone about a lawn-care service.

And one call that sent a chill down his spine. "Look around, hotshot. You think you're safe? Think again. Your perfect world is gonna end. Real soon."

The security system had been on when he returned. Nothing had been disturbed in the back entry, kitchen or dining room. Now, he backtracked and retraced his steps. Checked the windows, back door. The living room. Warren's bedroom. The two spare bedrooms. Everything was in place.

At the entry to the bedroom he used, the door stood ajar. He pressed two fingers against it and pushed it open. Reached inside for the light switch.

He hadn't exactly spent much time in there. He

hadn't made the bed and he'd left some shirts hanging over the back of a chair.

But now the drawers hung askew and his clothes were everywhere. He strode across the room and tested the lower locked drawer of his desk, his heart sinking as it easily pulled open. *Empty.*

He clenched his fists in anger at the violation. Someone had circumvented the security system, had been in this house and had willfully destroyed personal property.

Far worse, the laptop computer he kept at home was gone. And it held privileged information on clients as well as himself—a perfect source of information for identity theft.

If it fell into the hands of someone who could crack its security passwords, there'd be hell to pay.

He called 911 on his cell phone as he finished his search of the house, then he speed-dialed Jill. She answered, thank God, on the third ring. "Someone got past Dad's security system and broke in."

She drew in a sharp breath. "Are you okay?"

"The guy was long gone. The only room he tossed was mine, but now my laptop is missing. What he's got could mean real trouble, Jill."

"You did our taxes on it. Our investment records."

"There's enough information there to cause a hell of a lot of trouble for you, me and my clients."

"Have you called the sheriff?"

"He should be out here in an hour. Be careful, Jill. First it was just some stupid calls, then someone rear-ended your car. Now this."

"I've got Sadie, remember? The hundred-pound couch puppy? And this security system is newer than Warren's. He chose budget, you and I chose the best we could find."

"Still…" He thought for a moment, remembering what had happened the *last* time he'd stayed over-night at Chapel Hill. "Do you have anyone you could ask to stay with you?"

"Really, Grant. We've been through all of this before."

"One of the nurses at the hospital?" he insisted. "Donna? If not, I'd be glad to come up."

"Good *night,* Grant." She disconnected.

He paced the house, irritable and impatient, his uneasiness growing as the minutes ticked slowly past. As soon as the sheriff left, he was going up to Chapel Hill, whether Jill liked it or not.

It was on his third round through the main floor of the house that he saw the folded piece of paper propped on the fireplace mantel. A piece of paper that hadn't been there yesterday when he'd managed a cursory effort at dusting.

He picked it up by the edge and opened it care-fully to avoid smudging any possible fingerprints.

The room dropped a good fifty degrees as he

read the printed note inside…words that nearly stopped his heart.

> You destroyed my life and someday soon I'll be returning the favor. Nice bonus, seeing as how your little wife is pregnant. You might want to kiss her goodbye.

Grant alternated between shock, anger and fear for Jill's safety as he took Bitter Creek Road at sixty miles an hour. He'd dialed both her home and cell phones on his way out to his car, but there'd been no answer. Even now, someone could be at Chapel Hill.

Perhaps he'd already broken in to the house.

Grant white-knuckled the steering wheel and held his breath as the SUV hit an icy patch, fishtailed and ricocheted off a high snowbank the plows had built along the edge of the lane.

But beyond the adrenaline rush, beyond the urgency of this moment, was a more chilling question. If the stalker's information was correct, how could he possibly know?

AT THE SOUND of banging on the front door, Badger dug in his claws, leaped from Jill's lap and raced out of the parlor. Sadie erupted into a frenzy of barking—from a safe vantage point beneath the dining room table, Jill noticed, as she stepped warily out into the hall.

Her pulse raced as she fingered the cell phone in the pocket of her heavy robe. Grant had warned her, but she'd brushed his concern aside. Perhaps she'd made a very, *very* stupid mistake.

"Jill—it's me!"

She moved quickly to the entryway, adjusted the towel wrapped around her damp hair and pulled the door open to a blast of cold air. Sadie bounded down the hall to her side, wiggling and whining for Grant to pet her.

Relief at seeing a familiar face made Jill feel almost giddy, too. "We've got to stop meeting like this," she murmured, standing aside to let him in.

Ignoring her weak attempt at lightening the moment, he came in, sorting through his keys. "I thought for sure I still had a house key on this ring, but maybe not."

"Just as well. If you'd walked in and suddenly appeared in the parlor, I would have had a stroke."

She offered to take his coat but he just tossed it over the bench at the door. "You didn't answer your phones."

"That's what this is about?" She stared at him, incredulous. "I was in the *shower* until a few minutes ago, for heaven's sake."

"I told you about the phone message and my missing laptop. After we hung up, I ran across something else…a damn good reason to get up here."

Mystified, she tied her belt tighter as she followed him to the kitchen. "What, you want supper?"

"I want better lighting." He pulled an envelope out of his shirt pocket. "But first, I want to know if there's anything you have to tell me."

His accusing tone rankled. "I'm not on a witness stand, in case you haven't noticed."

"So you have nothing to say. *Nothing.*"

Her temper rose. "I can say that I resent playing games almost as much as your attitude. How's that, for starters?"

A muscle ticked at the side of his jaw as he withdrew a slip of paper from the envelope, carefully handling it by the edges as he unfolded it. "The sheriff is on his way here, and I don't care what you think, I'm staying at Chapel Hill until this guy is caught. In the meantime, maybe you owe me an explanation. If this is true, why the hell didn't you bother to tell me?"

Her body—her brain—went numb as she read the message. The revelation about her pregnancy was almost as chilling as the threat against her. *My God.*

Grant must have read the guilt on her face, because his voice dropped another fifty degrees and his eyes glittered with anger. "Then again, maybe this baby isn't mine."

CHAPTER SEVENTEEN

JILL STARED AT the man she'd once loved with all her heart. "I can't believe you said that."

"Is it true?" his voice was cold, dead calm.

"What? Am I pregnant?" she snapped. "Or are you asking if I sleep around?"

"Jill—"

"I'm not sure you deserve either answer. I want you out of this house, Grant. Now."

He looked down at her fingers trembling on the knot of her robe, then searched her face. "So it's true. After all our years together. After all the time I wanted us to start a family, and met complete resistance at every turn. After a miscarriage that nearly broke my heart. Why, Jill? Why now?"

"So...you think I *intentionally* got pregnant? Possibly with some bozo off the street, because just anyone would do." She felt her temper rising. "And I'm stupid enough to do something like that...on a whim?"

"I didn't say that."

"Oh, yes you did…or almost. I really don't want you here."

He braced his palms on either side of the note. "You *really* don't have a choice. We're still married. I'm still half owner of this place. And if you'll look at this a little closer, you'll realize that I'm only here for your own good." He glanced at his watch. "In a few minutes the sheriff will be here, too."

She gripped the back of a chair to still her shaking hands. "What's he going to do, guard the door with his guns drawn?"

"I'm giving him this letter. I've got a folder of various documents signed by several of the clients who seem like good suspects, so maybe he can have the state crime lab run the prints and find a match." Grant jingled his keys. "I'm also giving him a house key, so he can check out the damage at my dad's house and write up a report on that laptop."

Some of her anger dissipated at the reminder of just how far the intruder had gone. If it was the same guy in every case, he wasn't only highly motivated and persistent, but he was upping the stakes.

"You win. Make yourself at home. Do what you want. Just let Sadie out before you turn in, because I'm going to bed."

"Not so fast." He tossed a single house key onto the table and pocketed the rest. "I still haven't heard any real answer from you, and that's hardly fair."

She'd wanted to wait. Several weeks, maybe, in case there were problems that precluded the need to say anything at all.

Now she realized it was all an excuse, and for the first time could truly empathize with the teenagers who got knocked up on a first date. She hadn't thought this could happen to her. She could barely believe it. And the words simply caught in her throat.

"Well?"

"Yes. I'm pregnant. And yes, it's yours. *Satisfied?*"

His lips twitched. "Back then, yes." His flash of humor quickly faded. "But we were more than careful that night. There wasn't a *moment* that we weren't protected."

"You surely know the statistics. No matter what form of protection you use, there's a failure rate. With condoms, it's—"

He held up a hand. "I don't need a lecture."

"Okay, then. Let me promise you this. I'm the one carrying this baby, and there's no way I would consider terminating the pregnancy. None."

"That's not—"

"Let me finish. If you're concerned about financial obligations—yes, you get to share them for the next twenty-odd years. I'll have DNA tests to prove it. If you're worried about custody issues, I'd be happy with full custody, so this shouldn't hamper your new, single lifestyle."

He drew back as if she'd slapped him. "I don't deserve that."

"Actually, I think you do. You charge in here, slam a piece of paper on the table and demand answers. You essentially accuse me of sleeping with someone else, because *surely* this baby couldn't be yours."

"How the hell would any man react?" He rubbed a hand wearily over his face. "I'm sorry. It's been a difficult evening. I think you can allow me that much. Out of the blue, I learn you might be pregnant—and that some bastard is threatening to do you in. And I realize that if you *are* pregnant—and the baby's mine—you haven't even bothered to tell me. The next question would be whether or not you ever planned to."

"Eventually. It would be your legal right. But think whatever you want to. Stay here, if you wish. Just stay away from me."

THE SHERIFF ARRIVED twenty minutes later to pick up the house key and Grant's documents. He returned to Chapel Hill several hours afterward, his face grim. He stood just inside the front door, his coat dusted with snow and his hat in his hands.

"We had some guys from the DCI here on another case, and I brought them in on this one," he said. "They went through your dad's place looking for evidence and fingerprints."

"Any luck so far?"

"Hard to say. My best guess is that our guy thought to wear gloves and didn't leave a trace."

"And the computer?"

"I had my secretary send out a fax to all the pawnshops in the county, and to the stores that carry used computer equipment. I don't figure it'll turn up, though. This guy skipped the digital cameras, DVD player and the cash on your bureau, so he's got a plan for that laptop. Personal information, most likely."

"I'll call my clients tomorrow and warn them to watch for any activity in their accounts. I'll need to follow up on my personal investments, too."

"I wish I had an extra man to post up here. Leastways, every night."

"I'm staying."

"Don't blame you a bit. I know you and the doc don't exactly live together anymore. But with a new little one on the way, maybe you can work things out, eh?"

"Right." About as much of a chance that Sadie would turn pink and fly, but Grant forced a smile. "How soon can you get some answers?"

Randy settled his cap on his head and reached for the doorknob. "It's sure not like what you see on those TV shows. Could be weeks. Even months. But I promise, I'll let you know the minute I hear anything."

AFTER A SILENT and very awkward breakfast, Grant insisted on driving Jill to the clinic the next morning, but she refused.

On the chance that she might have an emergency call at the hospital, lack of immediate transportation could waste valuable time. But beyond that, the thought of being not only dependent, but trapped in the car with him, made her jittery.

He compromised by following her into town and extracting a promise that she would call him whenever she left the clinic.

When, she wondered as she hung up her coat in her office, had things gone so horribly wrong between them?

There couldn't be a more responsible, caring man than Grant. They'd shared what she'd thought was a perfect marriage…and then, piece by piece, things started to break down.

And now, they were at war. Subtly, of course. With the cool distance and careful conversations that—until last night—had insulated them from the deeper, darker emotions.

But last night he'd been cruel, and she'd been a shrew. And it had never been more clear that their relationship was beyond repair.

Donna poked her head around the corner. "Lost in thought?"

"I guess." Jill stowed her purse in a drawer and reached for the lab coat hanging on the hall tree.

"You haven't seemed like yourself lately. Are you feeling all right?"

Jill hesitated for a second, debating how much to share, but ultimately her nurse would find out anyway. She managed a faint smile. "With the exceptions of a massive hormonal shift, a death threat and World War Three in my personal life, I'm just dandy."

Donna chuckled as she moved into the doorway and leaned a shoulder against the frame. "Sounds like a major case of PMS to me."

"Not exactly. Are there any patients in the waiting room yet?"

"Two, and one waiting in the first exam room."

"Come on in and shut the door."

Donna's eyes widened. "Mary, Mother of God. You're *serious?*"

She shut the door and sank into one of the chairs by Jill's desk. Her eyes grew even wider as Jill quickly told her about the stalker, the pregnancy and the fact that Grant had shifted into full-scale protector mode.

Her fingertips pressed to her lips, Donna cast a nervous glance toward the door. "No wonder you've been edgy. Are you sure you should even be here? What if this guy just walks right in?"

"I don't think he'd be that careless about witnesses. There've been no clues about his identity. Every call has been made at night and traced to a public telephone outside a convenience store, where he could hide in the shadows. The state DCI is checking prints right now, but I'm convinced this guy wouldn't leave any." Jill took a deep breath. "So, if he actually does make a move, I figure he'd be smart enough to choose an isolated area. Possibly up at Chapel Hill."

"That's…that's *awful*. Just waiting and wondering. How can you *stand* it?"

"The sheriff is keeping tabs on my place and Grant insisted on moving in, so I'm hardly alone. And—" Jill folded her arms over her waist "—I've got a few other things on my mind as well."

"No kidding. Hey, congratulations—I think."

"Congratulations are welcome, but I'd rather not have the news get out just yet."

Donna nodded as she rose and turned to leave. "Got it."

"Oh, and Donna? If you hear or see anything suspicious…"

"I'll let you know right away," the nurse said fervently. "No doubt about that."

"It's been two weeks, Grant. Honestly, I think you could go home. And you can definitely stop escorting me to work."

"Ever the gracious hostess," he murmured. He looked at her over the edge of the sports section of the newspaper. "But it hasn't been so rough, has it? We see each other maybe fifteen minutes a day, tops."

"We've managed." Stepping over Sadie, who usually curled up at Grant's side, Jill gathered their plates and silverware from the table and headed to the kitchen. After loading the dishwasher, she stared at her reflection in the window above the sink.

The woman looking back at her appeared drawn. Tense. Not that it was any surprise.

It hadn't been an easy two weeks, watching for a threat that might never be realized. Scanning the parking lot before she stepped out of the clinic or hospital. Feeling alarm if the phone happened to ring, or an envelope appeared in the mail without a return address.

And then there'd been the awkward silences.

She and Grant had been painfully polite these past two weeks. He'd apologized and so had she, but there was something unnerving about living in a house with a man who'd once shared her bed. They both moved cautiously. Avoided the chance touch or glance that might be misconstrued.

Yet when her morning sickness had hit with a vengeance last week—the twenty-four-hour-a-day variety—he'd hovered, bringing her decaf tea and crackers, making supper every night. He shoveled snow and tended to Badger's litter box, and let Sadie in and out…and in and out.

Their conversation remained as stilted as ever, but he was becoming entirely too indispensable and it scared her a little. Before long, Warren would be back and then Grant would leave for his new condo and his new life. And he'd reminded her just how good it was to have someone else living in this house. Even if they had different goals, different outlooks on life and had said words that could never be recalled, the presence of another human being was reassuring.

A sudden, bone-chilling breeze swept through the kitchen. Shivering, she glanced at the still curtains, then double-checked the back door before going to the parlor, where she'd left her heavy wool sweater on the rocking chair.

Badger, never one to miss a warm place, had curled up on it. He gave her a baleful look as she lifted him and swiped his bed. "Sorry, bud. You've got a fur coat, and I don't."

She set him on the floor and turned to leave, but once again she felt an icy draft. The vagaries of an old, poorly insulated house. Nothing more than—

Her gaze dropped to the floor by the rocking chair. The *journal?*

She'd set it out to dry in the kitchen almost a month ago, and it had vanished. Janet, her once-a-month cleaning lady, had sworn she hadn't seen it, but as good-hearted as the woman was, she did tend to pick up and misplace things in odd places.

But Janet wasn't due until next week, and the book certainly hadn't been here yesterday.

"Grant?" Jill picked it up and walked to the dining room where he was still reading. "Where did you find this?"

He lowered the paper. "What is it?"

"An old book. I've looked everywhere for it, and just found it in the parlor."

"I've never seen it before." He frowned and searched her face. "You look a little pale. Are you all right?"

"I…I'm fine. Just surprised, that's all. Maybe Sadie liked the musty scent and took it somewhere. She's always hiding her chew toys." Jill held the book low enough for the dog to sniff at it. "You like this?"

Sadie sneezed and pulled away.

Grant brushed a fingertip across the cracked leather binding. "It's certainly old."

"It's a journal dating back to the 1800s. It might have belonged to the woman who built this place, but why would such an old treasure appear, then disappear and just as suddenly reappear? After all the owners who've been through here, you'd think one of them would have nabbed it."

"The carpenter was working way back under the

eaves after that tree fell. Maybe it was tucked way out of sight all these years."

"Of course." Except the man had firmly denied it. She turned to go back to the parlor. "I don't imagine it's exciting reading—that first owner was a spinster who rarely left home."

Grant laughed. "You never know. She might have led a double life."

In the parlor, Jill settled on the sofa under her afghan and switched on the stained glass lamp on the end table. The bulb, glowing through panes of amethyst, garnet and emerald glass, bathed the room in soft warm light that seemed to draw her into the past as she lifted the cover of the book and started to read.

The spidery script, written over a hundred years ago, was smudged in places…almost as if tears had fallen while the author wrote.

As Jill leafed through the pages, it became all too clear this woman hadn't led Grant's idea of an exciting life. Faye had faced tragedy. Loneliness. Heartache. And she'd been a veritable prisoner of this place until the day she died.

But *why?*

CHAPTER EIGHTEEN

JILL LAY IN bed, staring up at the ceiling for hours, imagining Faye in this very room—also lying alone. Waiting for a beloved fiancé who would never return.

Sure, the wallpaper was different now. New area rugs brightened the hardwood floors. But the pressed tin ceiling was original. Had Faye also counted those squares and fleur-de-lis swirls when sleep eluded her?

Drawn back to the journal, Jill started back at the beginning, reading more slowly this time. Absorbing the words, the emotions, the stubborn refusal of Faye Williston to accept the truth about her missing fiancé, even as the weeks and months rolled by.

Maybe the strength of that woman's determination accounted for the oppressive air of loneliness that lingered in the house.

Just your imagination. Nothing more than lack of sleep and changing hormones.

She set the journal aside and switched off the light.

But she couldn't stop thinking about the vehicle that had bumped her car. Faye. And the fact that someone, somewhere, just might want her dead.

GRANT STOOD AT the kitchen counter when Jill walked in the next morning, a cup of coffee in his hand. "You look awful," he said, taking a swallow. "Did you get any sleep at all?"

She shook her head. "Too much to think about, I guess."

"Find the directions to any buried treasure in that journal?" He lifted his cup toward the double windows facing the broad expanse of backyard, where dawn had tinted the snow a soft shade of rose. "She certainly would've had plenty of space for it."

"No treasures. Not so far, anyway."

He set aside his cup and leaned against the counter, his arms folded. "I'm calling the sheriff again today. There's still been no word from the DCI about those fingerprints."

Her stomach still queasy even after eating a handful of crackers from the box she kept by her bed, Jill moved to the refrigerator and pulled out a jug of cold water. "It's only been two weeks. I'm sure this isn't a high priority."

"It should be. They ought to be *preventing* crime instead of trying to figure it out after the fact."

She could see the strain in the fine lines at the

corners of Grant's eyes, and knew this whole situation hadn't been any easier for him than it had for her.

He had to be counting the days until they could go their separate ways once again.

She searched for a neutral topic. "What's your new condo like?"

"Just—a place to live."

"Pretty?"

"Bare. Utilitarian."

"Sounds a little depressing."

"No, it suits me very well." He glanced around at the froufrou curtains that had come with the place. The faded wallpaper, strewn with cabbage roses, they'd planned to replace when they started redecorating. "It's not quite as overwhelming."

"Then you're looking forward to getting back to Kendrick, and getting back to normal."

"Normal has a whole new meaning now," he said, glancing at her flat belly. His voice was rough when he added, "Especially come November."

They'd carefully skirted that issue along with just about everything else of any consequence since he'd arrived at Chapel Hill to stay. It had hung like a cloud between them. Nebulous. Unsettling.

"I *would* have told you about this on my own, Grant."

He nodded and pushed away from the counter. "I know."

She watched him cross the room. "And whatever you think—you *know* we tried to be careful. I had no intention of this happening."

"I'm sure you didn't. You always made your feelings perfectly clear on *that* topic." He hesitated at the doorway, then turned back to face her. "What I don't understand is your announcement that you plan to raise this child yourself. Where did that come from? When did you ever want children?"

Stunned, she stared at him. "I—"

"If it's just some sort of retaliation against me, I hope you realize I'd never relinquish my rights." Under the gentle tone, his voice held a thread of steel. "I'll fight you in court if I have to."

"That's never been my intent." She waved him away with a bored flip of her hand. "I was simply letting you off the hook."

"Good. And by the way, I have to be gone for the next two nights. If you're truly concerned about the baby's welfare, I'd advise you to call Donna or Grace and arrange to stay in town. Better than being out here alone." He tapped a case clipped on his belt. "If you need me for anything, I have a replacement cell phone, finally."

A moment later she heard the jingle of keys, and the front door slammed.

If you're truly concerned?

Feeling as if she'd been broadsided by an

eighteen-wheeler, Jill sagged against the kitchen table. Over the past weeks Grant had been caring. Attentive. No one could've asked for more through bouts of morning sickness.

He hadn't been *affectionate,* exactly, though her feelings had been softening toward him with every passing day. Yet beneath that nurturing facade he'd never had any real concern for her. Only for the baby growing inside her. She'd been a fool.

And that was something she wouldn't forget.

OVER THE LUNCH break at her clinic, Jill casually asked Donna about her week and discovered she had plans with her brother for dinner that night, and a meeting in the evening tomorrow.

And a few minutes ago, during her rounds at the hospital, she learned Grace had a hospital meeting and a high school open house that took care of both nights. Which left the bed-and-breakfasts in town—all closed for the winter season—and a mom-and-pop motel closed for renovation.

So much for Grant's idea, Jill thought as she finished the last chart and stowed it away on the shelf at the nurse's station.

Sure, she could've still asked one of her other friends or even stayed with Grace or Donna despite their other plans. But with Sadie and Badger at home it wasn't as if she'd be *alone.* And Sadie would certainly appreciate her reprieve from the pen Jill had arranged in the garage.

Marcia, one of the second-shift RNs on duty, looked up from her own charting and smiled. "You look a little distracted, Dr. Edwards. Everything all right?"

"Perfectly. I think I'll be sending Mrs. Graham home tomorrow, and probably Wade Foster. We'll need to have the social worker find a placement for Wade—at least for a while."

"Sounds like a great idea. His wife's been worrying about handling him while he's in that wheelchair." Marcia tapped a pen against her lower lip. "We saw one of Dr. Reynolds's patients last night for false labor again. Fast as her baby came last year, she doesn't want to take any chances. She's at forty weeks and counting every minute."

"I'm on call tonight if anything happens."

"I sure hope I'm on duty when she does go into labor. We don't get to deliver all that many babies here." One of the call lights started flashing at the desk. "That would be for me," Marcia murmured. "Good seeing you again, Doctor."

THE HOUSE SEEMED quieter than ever with Grant gone. Jill closed all of the curtains, reheated the fettuccine Alfredo he'd made last night and sat down to eat in the kitchen with Faye's journal opened on the table in front of her.

Sadie sat by her chair. The dog's mournful eyes followed every movement of Jill's fork.

"This is not your food, pal," Jill admonished her, reaching out to stroke her soft fur.

Sadie edged closer and managed to appear even more pathetically hopeful, until Jill finally gave her a bit of buttered toast. "I'm sure this is very bad for your training, but I won't tell if you don't. Deal?"

Sadie fixed her attention on the Granny Smith apple Jill quartered. "You do have a big pan of food over in the corner."

Sadie whined.

"And I have no idea what apples would do to your stomach. Aren't you supposed to be a carnivore?"

Doing her best to ignore those pleading eyes, Jill sipped at her decaf tea and started reading the faint, ornate script in the journal.

14 May 1881. I fear they'll come for me one day. But Jesse and I have prepared. What's gone will not be found, for the oak guards it well. We have goodly provisions stored to keep us until we are left in peace.

The entries had started off as any old journal, with snippets of information on health, maintenance of the livestock and the comings and goings of townspeople.

It relayed progress on the house as well—a process that apparently took more than eight difficult years with an endless list of tradesmen, carpenters who didn't show up and local contractors who didn't follow through.

On the worst days Faye's script formed deep slashes and angry scrawls on the page, and some of the entries didn't make sense. Perhaps even bordered on paranoia. Who, after all, would come after a veritable recluse? And why had she thought she needed to store provisions for a siege of some sort?

The rambling entry from the day before had even alluded to a hiding place "deep within," though what that meant was anybody's guess.

On other pages, the eloquent words and fanciful script related only the most innocuous events that filled her days. But whatever the mood, there was always an underlying loneliness. Sadness. And an inexplicable sense of guilt.

Now, whenever she passed the door to the cellar and felt that sudden eddy of chilled air, Jill imagined it a greeting from poor old Faye, and it didn't unsettle her nearly as much.

"I wish I could have met you," Jill murmured, shutting the book and setting it aside after she read the final entry. "I'll bet you had some stories to tell."

And perhaps they were in another volume. Surely Faye wouldn't have ended with the encampment of several strangers on the property without explaining what happened next.

Impatient and edgy, Jill wandered through the main floor of the house trying to guess at possible nooks and crannies that might have provided a secret hiding spot for Faye's other diaries.

The attic was a distinct possibility, and by day it would be possible to search there, given the light streaming through the fanciful eyebrow windows tucked under the eaves and cornices. At night, the dim lighting would make it impossible.

At ten o'clock, Sadie and Badger trooped up the stairs after her. They were welcome company, even when both of them leaped up onto her bed.

"Okay, you two. There's only room for two and I'm *not* the one sleeping on the floor."

Badger wasn't so bad. He snuggled under the top comforter near the foot of the bed and usually stayed all night.

Once she'd realized he wasn't going to suffocate and quit hauling him out from under the blanket every ten minutes, he'd proven to be a rather comforting foot warmer.

Sadie, on the other hand, felt she had to sleep crossways on the bed—in the middle—and tended to snore.

The hospital called at ten-thirty, right after Jill stepped out of the shower. She towel dried her hair, slipped into a warm sweater and slacks and hurried downstairs with Sadie at her heels.

"Grant's going to love this," she muttered to the dog after letting her outside one last time. She donned her down jacket and stepped into her insulated boots, then gave the returning dog a quick hug. "But we're just not going to tell him I had to go out, right?"

There was no choice, really. All the doctors took turns being on call, and this was her responsibility.

She left the main floor lights burning brightly, the curtains closed, and double-checked all the window and door locks before stepping outside.

Winter had stayed late this year, but the snow had been melting all week with temperatures that reached the mid-forties by day and dropped to just under freezing by night.

In a few places out in the open there were even patches of dark, moist earth, which scented the air with the promise of spring.

Breathing deeply, she scanned the yard and then hurried to her car, punched in the key code and climbed behind the wheel. She locked the door as soon as she closed it.

In twenty minutes she reached the E.R. entrance of the hospital, shucking her coat and gloves as she strode to the nurse's station.

Carl was one of the RNs on duty tonight. Young,

bright and often irreverent, he grinned at her. "Bet you hoped you wouldn't hear from me tonight."

"I *expected* to. What's up?"

He gestured toward the two open charts on the desk. "Anna's back, hoping she's going for the real thing tonight instead of more false labor. But her contractions slowed after she got here. Gwen is with her now. And the Bosworth boy just arrived. Drove his snowmobile into a fence post but probably didn't feel it much. The kid is flat drunk." Carl raised an eyebrow. "His mother is in there reading him the riot act, so I thought I'd give them a little space."

Jill began studying the boy's admission assessment. "How does he look?"

"Pupils are even, no lacerations or deep bruising. Blood pressure's good. The lab is running a CBC to check for evidence of internal bleeding. Tore through his snowmobile pants and scraped up the side of his thigh. He's going to have one hell of a hangover."

"I think I'll go in there and rescue him, then." Jill picked up the chart and followed the sound of a woman's angry voice to the third cubicle down from the desk. Pushing aside the curtain, she found the seventeen-year-old boy sitting on the gurney in a hospital gown, his head bowed.

For all her angry words, his forty-something mother appeared haggard and worried. "Oh, Dr. Edwards! I'm so glad you're here."

Jill moved to the opposite side of the gurney. "Hey, Randy. How do you feel?"

"Fine."

"Why don't you relax and I'll take a look. Does anything hurt?"

He shook his head as he lay back with a low groan. After checking his heart and lung sounds she examined his extremities, then palpated his liver and spleen.

As she continued her exam, she chatted casually, as much to calm his mother as to reassure him. "I don't suppose you'll be getting to ride much longer with spring just around the corner," she said as she helped him back up into a sitting position.

"A good thing, too," Mrs. Bosworth added. "That snowmobile is totaled anyway. The guys go out on the trails from one little town to the next hitting the bars. He's lucky to be alive. My ex buys him these expensive toys and doesn't think about what could happen."

Randy flinched at her words, but Jill mentally sided with his worried mother. She'd seen far too many fatal accidents involving alcohol and snowmobiles.

"I wasn't hitting all the bars. We were mostly west of town, up in the hills," he mumbled.

Where he must have been drinking with friends, given his bleary eyes and the beer on his breath.

Carl walked in and handed Jill the lab report, then gave Randy a wink as he left.

Jill checked the values. "I don't see any evidence

of internal bleeding so far—we'd see a drop in the hematocrit, and yours is normal." She clipped the report to his chart. "And I haven't found any evidence of deep bruising, fractures or head injury. Everything else seems fine."

"Praise be." Mrs. Bosworth's shoulders sagged with relief.

"I'll have Carl come in and clean up that abrasion for you, Randy," Jill said as she examined his thigh one last time. "We'll send you home with antibiotic cream and some extra dressing. Let us know if you notice heat, redness or increasing pain there. Any questions?"

He shook his head, but Mrs. Bosworth grabbed Jill's hand. "Thanks so much for coming in tonight. I can't tell you how worried I've been."

"No problem. Just keep an eye on him, and bring him back if you see any changes."

Out at the nurse's station Jill wrote her progress notes, then handed the chart to Carl. "The worry doesn't end, does it? First the pregnancy, when so many things can go wrong. Then the babies with SIDS and accident-prone toddlers…and teenagers learning to drive." She tipped her head toward the Bosworth cubicle. "And even later, when they're grown."

Carl chuckled. "You make it sound so depressing."

"Overwhelming, more like it. How's Anna doing?"

"Frustrated. She was two centimeters last night

and we sent her home. Now she's holding steady at three centimeters and not very happy about it."

"Has she had any bloody show yet?"

"Nope." Carl tapped the other chart sitting on the desk. "Vital signs all fine. Gwen had the fetal monitor on her and says the baby's heart is regular."

She'd attended close to a hundred births, but now every part of the process took on new meaning. *In November, this will be me.* "Sounds like we can send her home again. I'll look over her chart and then go talk to her."

The young woman on the bed blew at her bangs in frustration when Jill walked into the room. "I don't suppose you can just make this happen," she grumbled. "A little pill or something?"

Jill laughed. "I can imagine how you feel, but no. You're right at forty weeks and it ought to happen any day. When do you see your doctor next?"

"Friday. Which seems like an eternity away, right now." She levered herself up on the bed with her elbows. "I'm guessing this will never end. I'll go into labor, come here and everything will stop…no matter how many times. Like that movie about the guy who has to do the same day over and over."

"Let's take a look." Jill scrubbed up and donned vinyl gloves, then did a quick check of the woman's cervix. "Sorry. Carl was right. You're at three and holding. But who knows? Out of the blue, things could really start moving. You might even be back tomorrow."

"Please, let that be true. I feel like I'm carrying a hundred-pound sack of flour in this belly."

Jill laughed. "I can only imagine."

AFTER HER WEEKLY Thursday morning meeting at Ollie's Diner, Grace hurried back to the hospital.

Following a promising interview with a nurse wanting to move into the area, she buried herself in the hospital policy and procedure manuals—massive ring notebooks requiring annual revision and dated signatures.

A few weeks ago, even this mundane task would have seemed far more interesting. Everything in her life had taken on a brighter hue because, wonder of all wonders, Dan Travers had taken her to the lakeshore supper club for dinner and dancing that first night. And then he'd asked her out again and again and again.

They'd gone antiquing and had attended school events with Ross. They'd gone to the little church out in the country, with its pretty white steeple, and for long walks, breathing in the moist, sweet air of early April.

"Looks like you're having fun."

Grace shook off her reverie and looked up at Erin Reynolds, standing in the door. "Nope, but all of this has to be done before I can retire."

"Is anything wrong?"

"No…just thinking." Erin hesitated, her brows knitted with concern, but Grace waved her on. "I'll be fine."

She got back to work on the pharmacy cleaning schedules but soon smiled wistfully to herself, remembering the impromptu dance lesson Warren had given her before that first date.

He'd been so sweet to offer. So patient with her fumbling, awkward steps.

Ross had manned her old record player in the kitchen—once he figured out how to make it work—and cheered her on.

Warren had encouraged her, even when she tromped on his toes or found herself leading, until they'd dissolved in laughter that she'd somehow mixed up left and right the minute she stepped into his arms.

He'd helped her through a two-step, though. A slow waltz. An attempt at salsa that left them both breathless.

And because he was such a good friend, he'd made her first date with Dan a night to remember.

But despite one perfect evening after another, despite the attention of the man she'd dreamed of for so many years, some of Grace's initial joy had dimmed.

Unbelievably, she'd found herself hedging when Dan called…or discovering unavoidable delays.

It was just all too ironic. Dan was available. Interested. He'd been her gold standard for all gentlemen, and no one else had ever come close to measuring up.

Yet now she inexplicably found herself thinking about Warren. A man, still totally in love with his dead wife, who'd taken off for Florida, possibly for good, without so much as a farewell.

RAY KICKED A dent in the side of the old Mustang, then paced between the car and the rustic cabin he'd rented deep in the woods north of Blackberry Hill.

He'd followed Natalie for weeks, staying far behind her. Taking special pleasure in watching her. In the nervous flick of her gaze, the tension in her spine.

She'd sensed something, all right, and her anxiety filled him with a lovely sense of power and control. He'd enjoyed that game enough to extend it, wanting her to suffer. But he'd toyed with her too long.

Yesterday, she'd disappeared.

Last night he'd jimmied the lock on her apartment and found only the furniture and bare walls. At the salon, there'd been a Closed—For Sale sign posted in the window.

He'd been too careful for her to detect his presence. He'd never once caught her eye. Longer hair, glasses and scruffy clothes had worked perfectly.

But someone had warned her, and it wasn't too hard to guess who that was. That lawyer she ran to for every little thing…then flirted with until Ray's stomach churned.

Or the guy's wife. Had she noticed him last month

in Ollie's, the day she'd blabbed about her pregnancy to that other woman? Did she have any idea who he was?

Edwards was responsible for Ray's incarceration in Florida. He'd come between Ray and Natalie, and he was the bastard responsible for the divorce.

It was time. Natalie and Edwards were both going to pay.

CHAPTER NINETEEN

AFTER TWO COURT hearings, wading through a child custody dispute that nearly came to blows, and coming out of a restaurant after a late supper to find he had a flat tire, Grant wished for the relative peace of Blackberry Hill. Just one more night, and then he could go home. It would be a great relief.

Perhaps more so because he knew he'd been a complete jerk this morning. Jill hadn't deserved his accusations, and she sure as hell hadn't deserved his threat to fight her in court.

In fact, it was a miracle she hadn't thrown him out on his ear. He'd tried to call the house three times tonight but she hadn't picked up. Maybe she was screening his calls. He wouldn't blame her.

When he got back he was going to—

"Hey, you want me to call a wrecker?" Phil, who'd stayed in the restaurant to talk to a client, came out and lounged against the hood of Grant's car. He watched with mild amusement as Grant finished tightening the last of the lug nuts. "I know the guy at Mel's. If I tell him you're my brother, he'll give you a deal."

"Very funny." Grant lowered the jack and gathered the tools. He put them in the cab of the truck and tossed the flat in the back.

"Are you coming back in for a couple drinks?"

The thought held no appeal. "I think I'd better just turn in."

Phil cocked his head and frowned. "You sure don't look happy. Are things going okay?"

"It's good to be back at Dad's practice again. Most of the time, anyway. Have you heard from him lately?"

"At first, five, six times a day." Phil shrugged. "The past couple weeks, nothing more than a fast e-mail or two saying he was having a great time."

"Same here. Maybe he's finally learning to relax a little."

"He did mention finding something really special at some fund-raiser auction. Maybe he's found some cute little thing to help him spend his money."

Their eyes met as they both tried to imagine Warren flirting with *anyone*.

Grant rolled down his shirt cuffs and reached into the truck for his jacket. "Not likely. With Mom gone, he's probably just sitting in front of the TV watching golf all day."

"Maybe one of us should call." Phil jingled the

change in his pocket. "You'd have a better reason, since you're running his practice. He won't like it if he realizes we're checking up on him."

"Tomorrow afternoon then, when I'm in his office. I can think up a reason of some sort."

Phil grinned. "Let me know what he says." He glanced over his shoulder toward the restaurant. "I s'pose I'd better get in there again before Sandra gets ticked off. Making conversation with Allan Pearson can be quite a challenge."

Grant lifted a hand in farewell and slid behind the steering wheel. Making conversation with *any* of them felt like a challenge tonight, yet going to his empty condo wasn't appealing, either. But Blackberry Hill was two hours away and he had an early appointment here in the morning. It made no sense to go back.

He drove out of the parking lot and stopped at the highway.

To the right—home to Blackberry Hill.

To the left—back to the condo.

Setting his jaw, he turned on his blinker and pulled out into traffic toward the condo. He'd moved here last fall. Bought a place. Settled in and planned to make it permanent. So why did Blackberry Hill still feel like home?

It didn't take any effort to figure that one out. The problem was that he'd been busy burning bridges every chance he had.

Lost in thought, he almost missed the vibration of the phone at his belt. He grabbed it as he turned off the highway.

He hit the brakes at the first sound of the man's low, derisive laughter.

"Good timing, Edwards. Real nice of you to leave town."

"Who is this?" Backing into an awkward, one-handed three-point turn, Grant jammed his foot down on the accelerator and sped up to the highway. Skidded to a semi-stop and turned sharply to the right toward Blackberry Hill. "What do you want?"

"Just as perceptive as ever," the caller mused. "Still not figuring out a damn thing."

"Of course I don't know what this is about." Grant's heart slammed against his ribs as he floored the accelerator and fought to keep his voice calm. "So this game of yours is *meaningless.*"

"Oh, it has meaning to me. Are you tired of waiting for your reward?"

The white dashes down the center of the road melted into a solid strip of white when he hit sixty, then seventy miles an hour. White-knuckling the steering wheel, Grant cleared his throat. "I'm tired of hearing about something I want to fix but can't— because I don't know what's wrong. We could meet, you and I. Anywhere you like, just say the word. Maybe tonight?"

The caller gave a low, satisfied laugh. "I know what you're doing," he purred. "You figure you can stop the inevitable by keeping me on the phone. I imagine you must be on Highway 68 right now, pushing that truck of yours to the limit. But you know what? You're just too damned far away to make a difference." He disconnected.

Grant hammered a fist against the steering wheel, his blood pounding in his ears and a cold sweat trailing down his back. He called the Blackberry Hill sheriff's office, then tried to reach Jill again.

The caller was right. He was too far away. The two-hour trip might take a half hour less at top speeds, but the curves and gentle hills made it a no-passing zone nearly all the way.

If the sheriff and his two deputies had been called out clear across the county, it could take them a hell of a long time to arrive.

And right now, that bastard could be breathing down Jill's neck.

SOME DOCTORS RESENTED being called out of their beds at night.

But for Jill, there was always an adrenaline rush that made night calls to the hospital more exciting, as she anticipated what she would find. Wondered how she would meet the challenge. Night calls often meant high drama. High stakes. The chance to save a life.

The peaceful, dark and empty streets en route to the hospital were always in sharp contrast to the blazing lights and tension of the emergency department, where every one of her senses felt heightened.

Going home was a different story.

Now, stepping out into the quiet night, she nodded to the lone security guard smoking near the back door and walked slowly to her car. Drained, exhausted. Wishing only to crawl back under the covers.

The streets were slushy now, the remaining snowbanks a dirty gray that blended with the night. Outside of town, past the end of the streetlights, she drove slowly to absorb the peacefulness. The feeling of being the only person awake in the entire county.

She'd seen four patients tonight. After Anna and the Bosworth boy there'd been a man with mild chest pain and a baby with RSV, who'd both arrived just as she was getting ready to go home. A satisfying night. No serious injuries, but busy enough to be interesting.

At Bitter Creek Road she turned, and slowed even further as the car shimmied through deep slush interspersed with muddy patches before she started the final climb up the hill.

At the top she breathed a sigh of relief…and exhaustion. It would feel so good to have a nice hot chocolate, put on her warm flannel pajamas and just drift off to sleep.

She parked close to the house and cut the lights. Moonlight silvered the yard, leaving the towering pines dark as sentinels.

Inside the house she heard Sadie barking. It was reassuring, knowing that Sadie was on patrol, though Jill carefully scanned the yard before grabbing her purse and making a dash for the front porch.

Turning the key in the lock, she stepped inside. Sadie was still barking. *Frantically* barking now, and she wasn't looking at Jill.

The dog's eyes were fixed on the windows to the right of the door.

Jill's heart lodged in her throat and, her pulse hammering, she jerked the storm door shut just as a towering shape loomed out of the darkness.

With a sharp cry she slammed the inside door shut. Rammed the dead bolt home.

Collapsing against the door, terror washed though her like freezing rain.

Safe. For now.

But from the other side of the door came the sound of laughter…low and cruel.

And she knew it was only a matter of time.

GRANT CURSED AT the pickup in front of him. *Fifty miles an hour.*

He'd tried passing four times, even testing the boundaries of a no-passing zone once. Each time he reached a straight section of road, there were oncoming cars.

Turn off. Turn off, he growled, hitting the steering wheel again with the palm of his hand.

But like an old man, the rickety truck in front of him toddled along, braking now and then, weaving in its lane.

Precious minutes were ticking by. He'd called the sheriff's office twice, but with a major house fire on the far side of the county, it might be an hour before they made it back to town. Longer still before they could get to Chapel Hill.

And every passing second could be Jill's last.

A straight section of road opened up ahead.

Grant floored the accelerator and roared around the old truck; cutting in just as a triangular No Passing Zone sign appeared.

Finally. He sped to seventy-five, the trees passing by in a blur on either side of the road.

Outside Blackberry Hill he skidded to a half stop and squealed the tires as he turned up a back way to avoid the town itself. Gravel spat from beneath the tires like buckshot and he nearly lost control.

Another few miles. *Just a few more.*

At the far edge of town he cut back to the main highway and floored the accelerator. The bright red fuel light came on. *So close…*

Breathing hard now, he whipped around the turn

onto Bitter Creek Road, sending up a rooster tail of slush and snow behind him.

"Almost there, honey," he whispered. "Almost—"

The headlights picked up something gray ahead…a dry patch? He feathered the brakes to avoid spinning out.

It came up fast—*too fast*—something lying across the road?

He hit black ice. Skidded. The truck spun in dizzying circles. Then crashed head-on into a barrier across the road, metal screaming. Twisting. The airbags deployed, filling the cab with a cloud of white.

Shaken, he stared out the window at a massive log across the lane. It hadn't been there before. Hell, there hadn't even *been* any logs stacked in the area.

It had been brought in.

Arranged on the road.

And the person responsible was undoubtedly another two miles up…with Jill. Wincing, Grant released his seat belt and eased to the passenger side door.

And hoped like hell he could reach her in time.

JILL BACKED SLOWLY away from the front door, her gaze riveted to the knob and one hand on Sadie's collar.

Was it turning? Her heart battered against her ribs as she took another step back. Then another. Sadie's growls intensified. She tried to lunge for the door.

Reaching for the purse at her feet without taking her eyes off the door, Jill searched in it for her cell phone. With a cry of dismay she dropped to one knee and pawed through the purse. Was it in her lab jacket at the hospital? In her *car?*

Her palms cold and damp, she glanced up at the security system panel to make sure it was armed. Turning, she ran down the hall, dragging Sadie behind her.

The phone in the kitchen...she had to get there. She had no doubt that the man outside could get in the house. If not through the door, through a window— and there were dozens of them on the first floor.

Relief threatened to overwhelm her when she got to the kitchen. She grabbed the receiver.

Dead.

Stunned, she dropped the phone, leaving it to dangle loosely from its cord.

The stranger outside must've moved to the back of the house. She heard him rattle the back door. Kick it hard. Then again. Wood splintered. Glass shattered.

He kicked the door again, with enough force to shake the delicate chandelier overhead. He'd be through that door in seconds. Even now, he could be reaching through the broken glass to release the dead bolt.

And she was all alone.

CHAPTER TWENTY

SADIE BURST INTO A frenzy of barking at the sound of shattering glass and nearly wrenched free of Jill's grip on her collar. *Let her go now? Later?*

An inner voice told her not just yet. Jill hurried across the kitchen dragging the dog along. Sadie's claws scrabbled against the floor as she fought every step of the way. "No, girl—easy."

But where could they go?

When the security system's alarm went off the county sheriff would be notified, but with a three-man force and an entire county to cover, it could be hours before anyone arrived.

The intruder could search the house at his leisure. Toy with her while she was cornered. He'd be able to do whatever he wanted. Take whatever he wanted. Make sure there'd be no witness left behind.

She stepped out into the hallway. Shutting the door behind her, she struggled to shove a heavy oak table in front of it. It wouldn't hold him for long. A few seconds, maybe less.

She spun around, her panic rising. *The attic—the bedrooms—the parlor—there was no place safe. Not for long.*

A sudden cold breeze swept over her.

She turned slowly.

Faced the basement door.

The words from the old journal came back to her as if someone was speaking them in her ear.

I fear they'll come for me one day. But Jessie and I are prepared. We have goodly provisions…

She and Grant had been down in the dank, dirt-floored basement several times, but she'd never wanted to linger. The walls were piles of massive stones, the floor uneven. Heavy timbers supported the house, as well as the walls of a maze of empty storage rooms swathed in spiderwebs and choking dust.

A few low-watt lightbulbs hung on twisted brown cords while the rest of the cellar was dark as pitch.

The back door of the house crashed open. She heard footsteps creeping up the three inside steps leading to the kitchen.

Sadie erupted into another burst of frantic barking.

Stifling a cry of panic, Jill silenced the dog and took a tighter grip on her collar, then eased open the cellar door. Pushed the dog through into the pitch-dark onto the small landing on the other side and followed, closing the door behind them.

She reached into her pocket for the tiny penlight on her key ring and hurried down the stairs…every creak and groan of the wood as loud as a gunshot to her ears. Had the intruder heard? Would he thunder down the stairs any second and corner her here?

Sweeping the area with the flashlight, she tried to remember the layout of the storerooms. Like a rabbit warren, some of them led from one to another. Some were dead ends.

Sadie whined and tried to turn for the stairs. "It's okay," Jill whispered. She leaned down to hug the dog's massive neck. And then she felt it again—a cold draft, coming from the far right.

Her teeth chattering, she hesitated, then followed the chilly air…gingerly feeling her way with an extended hand. Ten, then fifteen feet down a narrow aisle. The rush of air filtered through a rotting door frame to her right.

She slowly twisted the filigree doorknob and eased the door open. She angled a thin beam of light into the empty storeroom. Directly across from the door, a sagging cupboard stood at a slight angle to the stone wall, its shelves askew and lower doors hanging open. Some empty casks had been heaped to one side, along with twisted lengths of metal that might have been some sort of 1800s farm equipment.

Jill took a deep breath, thankful for Sadie's comforting presence. If nothing else, maybe they could wedge behind that cupboard. A quick look revealed no lightbulb in the area, which would make it harder for someone to search.

Surely no one would guess she'd brave this nightmare of a cellar, much less be hiding back there.

Above, Jill heard heavy footsteps crossing back and forth on the main floor and her hand tightened on the dog. Then the footsteps sounded faster. Something shattered. The intruder thundered up the stairs to the second floor, she guessed, as the sounds faded away. It wouldn't take long to search the bedrooms and the attic.

And it wouldn't be long before he'd be down here.

"C'mon, girl, we'll be okay." Jill gingerly crossed the room. Something crunched underfoot—perhaps decades of old mouse droppings—and from the darkness she heard the thin, high-pitched squeal of a rodent.

Sadie barked sharply and tried to lunge at it.

Jill grabbed for her muzzle. *"No!"* she whispered, her heart pounding. Had the intruder heard?

In front of the cupboard she said a quick silent prayer and then stepped to one side, half afraid to look at what might be hidden there.

Another eddy of cold air swirled past her. Could it be…?

She eased a little farther in and hesitantly aimed her flashlight at the wall.

Her heart dropped. *Nothing.* Just more stone wall.

Yet…the air smelled of damp earth. Melting snow. And early spring.

She edged forward, still hanging on to Sadie's collar, and crouched down. The flashlight beam picked out empty darkness between some of the basketball-sized rocks, a cement-like substance between others.

What if…?

She curved her fingers around a stone and tugged.

Sand showered to the floor as it moved, just a few millimeters. *Moved.*

Her hands shaking, she looked over her shoulder at Sadie. "Sit!" she commanded. "Stay!"

The dog whined, trying to pull away from Jill's grasp toward the way they'd come.

The cellar door squeaked open. She heard someone step onto the creaky wooden landing.

In minutes the intruder would be in the basement. It wouldn't take him long to find her. And then…

"Please." She tried to quell the panic in her voice. "Good girl, Sadie. *Sit!"*

The dog sat, her body rigid and her eyes were fixed on the door behind them.

Frantic, Jill set the flashlight on the floor and pulled at the stones. Prayed that this was the place Faye had written about, where there could be escape.

Her pursuer descended the stairs slowly.

One step. Another. Faint light flickered intermittently through the rotted wooden door of the storeroom.

He was sweeping the main area of the cellar with the beam of his flashlight as he descended. Cautious. Careful. Thorough.

Breathing hard, her heart thundering in her ears. She pulled harder at the rock and suddenly it fell with a heavy thud at her knees.

Cool air rushed into the room as she threw all of her weight against the next rock, then another, until they tumbled into the dark place on the other side of the wall. *Almost enough space—but what waited on the other side?*

Sadie growled.

Someone was shuffling across the floor toward the storeroom. The sweep of light grew brighter. Closer.

She twisted and reached for the dog's collar but Sadie jerked away, the hair on her back raised. Her growl intensifying.

Blazing light filled the room. With a sharp cry Jill fell back against the wall, shielding her eyes with one hand. Sadie burst into furious barking, her jaws snapping as she launched at the man in the doorway.

He cried out in alarm. Something flashed silver in the darkness. A deafening shot rang out, reverberating through the stony caverns of the cellar.

Sadie yelped as she dropped in a motionless heap of black fur.

Horror slammed through Jill's chest and she blindly groped at the wall behind her.

The flashlight beam fixed on her face. Blinding her. "Well, well, well," the man's voice was low. Mocking. "How very convenient to find you down here."

She'd been frightened before. Now terror gripped her. The man holding the flashlight was tall—well over six feet. Burly. She'd never be able to fight him off. And that face—eerily lit in the glow of the flashlight—was evil. "W-who are you?"

"Someone who lost a great deal and is repaying the favor in spades."

The floor above them creaked. The soft sound of footsteps moved down the hallway above and stopped…by the door to the cellar? *Please God, let it be the sheriff.*

She edged back a few inches toward the break in the wall. "I don't understand. Please—whatever you want upstairs, take it—money, anything. Leave me alone and I'll never tell anyone. I promise."

"It's you I want, sugar. Only you." He strolled to the center of the room, his voice taking an odd, crooning rhythm. "Your husband is on his way here, and I'll have a little surprise for him, too. People will think you two have just gone off on a nice trip somewhere."

She heard a faint creak of the cellar stairs.

Someone else was coming.

If this man had a buddy joining him, her chances would drop to zero. Even if it was the sheriff, he was clearly upstairs and this guy was only a dozen feet away.

She eased onto the balls of her feet. Tensed. Then pivoted and threw herself through the small hole in the wall. Into perfect, impenetrable darkness.

The dirt floor felt damp and cold beneath her knees and palms. Here the air was much colder—the current stronger. Dankness and an odd, moldy odor surrounded her like a moist blanket but she plowed on, hoping—praying—for an escape route.

Her hands bumped some sort of sticks that clattered together. Something metal, long and cold.

And then she hit a wall of earth and stone. Patting at it, looking for a way to get out, she rose to her knees, then to her feet. She could hear the rush of winter wind outside, now—above. Way, way above her head. Shaking from the cold she turned awkwardly, feeling for a ladder. Praying for steps. *Nothing.*

Behind her she heard the man grunt. Heard the heavy thud of rocks as he cleared a wider hole in the wall.

A moment later he stood inside the earthen chamber. His flashlight swept through the narrow cave and zeroed in on her. "Well, my dear. You certainly aren't going anywhere now."

Her heart in her throat, she glanced wildly to the left and right, but saw only solid earth walls. Then she looked down at her feet—and drew a sharp breath.

Her pursuer moved closer, his gun hand steady. "Your husband ruined my life, you know. He destroyed everything that mattered, and now—"

"Jill? Jill!" Grant's voice echoed through the cellar. "Are you down here?"

The intruder hesitated, glanced over his shoulder. In that split second she grabbed the metal object at her feet and rushed forward. Swung with every ounce of strength she possessed.

The man screamed. His flashlight and gun flew out of his hands and he fell against the wall, clutching his arm.

Before he could regain his feet she'd grabbed the gun and the light and had both aimed at his doughy face. "If you even twitch, I'm pulling this trigger," she snapped. "And believe me—after what you did to my dog—I'd be happy to do it."

"Jill!" Grant's voice was closer now. Frantic.

Relieved to hear the blessed sound of his voice, she called out, "Yes! Back here."

The gun still aimed at the man on the ground, Jill sidestepped across the cavern. When Grant emerged from the opening, she fought the urge to throw herself into his arms. "I can't believe you're here! I was terrified! This guy—he broke in, and he said he was going to—"

"I know, I know."

"And Sadie—"

"I think she's going to be okay, Jill." He held her close for a long moment, and she felt so safe, so protected that she never wanted to leave his embrace. But at a low groan from the man who'd doubled up over his arm, she took a step back. "I hit him pretty hard. I…guess I should take a look."

"Not until we tie him up. I think I saw some sash cord back by the stairs."

Grant went after it, turning on the cellar lights on his way. Weak illumination filtered through the warped plank wall of the room and gilded the swooping, matted spiderwebs hanging in the corners.

He came back a minute later and secured the man's wrists to his leather belt. "This ought to hold, though I don't think he'll be going anywhere too fast."

Jill edged closer to stare down at him. And for the first time, got a good look at his face. Was this the man who'd bumped into her at Ollie's? She'd asked several times, but the waitress had never seen him again. Had he been stalking her all this time?

Her stomach started to feel queasy. "I don't understand. He wanted to kill me, and I don't even know who he is."

AN HOUR LATER the sheriff drove away with the intruder in handcuffs.

Jill sat on the settee in the parlor, beyond exhausted. Her fingers, she noted with a sense of detachment, were still trembling. "Ray was a client of yours?" she repeated.

"*He* wasn't. It was his ex-wife. He's an abusive, manipulative and dangerous man, and she was terrified of leaving him last fall." Grant paced to the front windows, then back to the fireplace. "I had to meet her at odd times when he was away."

"Natalie."

Grant nodded. "Thing is, even after the divorce she never would've been safe with him still in town. When I finally convinced her to report his spousal abuse to the police, they found outstanding warrants on him in Florida. He tried to run, but the cops picked him up in the next county."

"That rankled, I'm sure."

"Sure it did. He lost a prized possession—his wife. He was taken to jail in Florida. He lost his job up here. I'm guessing that he wasn't all that balanced in the first place, and this just set him off."

She'd left Faye's journal here this morning—a lifetime ago—and now she traced a finger across the brittle binding. "It's ironic, really…I imagined spirits in this house…but that cold, eerie draft was nothing more than an air current drawn into the cellar when the wind is just right."

"Yet if you hadn't known about that hiding place, Ray might have found you before I could get here."

"Something I don't even want to think about." Jill shivered, remembering the man's derisive laugh.

With Ray's hands bound, she'd tended to the wound on his shoulder—from the rusted Civil War sword she'd found on the floor.

Later, she and Grant had searched the cavern and they'd found the partial skeletal remains of someone who'd apparently been buried there…his corroded brass military buttons scattered among the bones. And in a small, sealed casket, they found the final volume of Faye's diary.

"I—I'm too exhausted to even think straight any longer," Jill murmured. "I…guess you don't have to worry about staying here any longer."

Grant held her gaze as he crossed the room to her. "I know it's late. We can talk more tomorrow. But I need you to know one thing."

She stood, swallowing hard. "And that is?"

"That I would do anything, *anything* to keep you safe. I cannot imagine a world without you in it, and when I look back at the mistakes I made during our marriage, I wish I could go back and have one more chance to do it right."

"Mistakes? I think they were mostly mine." She managed a faint smile. "How wrong was it for you to want a family?"

"While I expected you to put everything you wanted on the back burner." He rested his hands on her shoulders. "I said unforgivable things to you Monday morning…and probably a dozen other times as well. I just want you to know that I'm sorry. That I'll do better. And I'd do anything if I could take back those words."

She saw the pain and love and tentative hope in his eyes that mirrored her own emotions. "Maybe we both need to try harder. Every day. In twenty or thirty years we might even get it right."

The laugh lines at his eyes deepened. "Maybe so."

And then he lowered his mouth to hers in a kiss that reminded them of every reason they should try.

EPILOGUE

JILL LEANED BACK against Grant's chest, his arms
around her, as they stood on the front porch at
Chapel Hill.

"It couldn't be a more perfect day," she whispered, looking out over the profusion of vintage roses
blooming in the garden. "Do you suppose Faye
planted those flowers?"

"Maybe. I do know you're right—this day is
perfect." He kissed the side of her neck. "But that's
because of you, and the fact that this time we're
going to make our marriage work."

Purple hollyhocks and cheery little Shasta daisies
swayed in the June breeze, fresh with the delicate
scent of the flowers and the pine forest that rimmed
the lawn. Along the house, the pink fairy lilies had
come into bloom just yesterday, adding masses of
frothy color.

The guests were arriving for the renewal-of-vows
ceremony that Grant had suggested back in April.

Relatives and close friends wandered through the grounds bending to admire the flowers, or stood back to shade their eyes against the sun as they studied the work being done on the house.

The painters had redone the house in its original pale yellow, with crisp, sparkling white for the gingerbread trim and spindled porches.

Barb had come with Patsy's children, and stood watching over them as they played catch with Sadie. They burst into laughter as once again Sadie returned the ball to little Zoe—it didn't matter who threw it.

And over by the daylilies, Warren stood talking to Grace, of all people. He'd arrived home two days before the wedding, his face a mask of grim duty…until he ran into Grace at the rehearsal and discovered Dan was no longer in the picture.

He offered Grace the crook of his elbow and they strolled up the walk arm in arm, looking for all the world like a pair of young lovers despite the silver in their hair.

Grace wore a pretty lilac dress and matching sandals, and it was hard for Jill to even remember that first impression of her as a stern and forbidding force to be reckoned with at the hospital.

"Are you two going to be next?" Jill teased.

Grace blushed. "Maybe. We're thinking about a private little ceremony somewhere, then a trip to Hawaii. I've never been there."

Her heart overflowing with joy for her old friend, Jill gave her a long hug, then shook Warren's hand. For all the years Grace had given of herself to countless foster children and to the patients and staff of the hospital, she deserved this so much. "I'm just thrilled for you both."

"We've asked Ross to stay on with us," Warren said. "He's happy here and is doing so well we couldn't imagine sending him back to his mother."

"That's wonderful." Jill grinned at them. "So you two get to step right into the 'parenting of teenagers' role. Some would say that's a challenge."

"Not with a boy like Ross." Grace looked over her shoulder to the people just arriving. Ross was among them, with a pretty young girl at his side.

"There's raspberry punch and wine set up by the springhouse," Jill said. "Will you all stay for supper afterward?"

Grace nodded and drifted off with Warren's arm threaded through hers.

"Are you ready, Mrs. Edwards?" Grant curved an arm around Jill's shoulders. "I think everyone is here."

"I need to go inside. For just a moment."

"You aren't having second thoughts, right?"

"Never." She kissed him lightly on the cheek and turned away, lifted the hem of her lacy blue dress and walked up the porch steps.

Inside, the house was quiet. She still felt that chilly draft now and then, though the workman had sealed off the secret cavern in the cellar.

Had that secret grave been the reason Faye had been so afraid to leave the house? So determined to keep watch over her property, fearing someone might discover her dark secret? The second volume of the diary had offered no clues about the identity of the skeleton, only that the man had looted the house and had tried to rape Faye. Somehow, in the struggle, she'd managed to drive a knife into his belly.

And so she had lived on in this house, longing for a lover who never returned. Filled with guilt over the death she'd caused, with the grisly evidence hidden beneath her home.

"Your secrets are safe," Jill whispered. She turned to go and found Grant waiting at the front door. His smile flashed white against his tanned, handsome face, and his eyes were filled with emotion that brought tears to her own.

As she stepped into his arms, a warm breeze caressed her skin, and a feeling of peace settled over the old Victorian house like a gentle benediction.

"I think we've broken the curse," she whispered. "We've proved that love doesn't always die."

He kissed her. The long, slow, seductive kind of kiss

that promised long, hot nights and a lifetime of commitment. A chance to start over, and make things right.

And then they walked out into the sunshine to join the waiting crowd.

HARLEQUIN®

Super Romance

MARRIAGE
IN JEOPARDY
by Anna Adams

SR #1336

On the surface, Josh and Lydia Quincy
have it all—a nice house, a baby on the way,
work they both love. But one tragic act
reveals cracks that cannot stay hidden.

It's where you belong.

On sale March 2006

*Available wherever
Harlequin books are sold!*

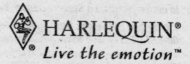

If you enjoyed what you just read,
then we've got an offer you can't resist!

Take 2 bestselling
love stories FREE!

Plus get a FREE surprise gift!

Clip this page and mail it to Harlequin Reader Service®

IN U.S.A.	IN CANADA
3010 Walden Ave.	P.O. Box 609
P.O. Box 1867	Fort Erie, Ontario
Buffalo, N.Y. 14240-1867	L2A 5X3

YES! Please send me 2 free Harlequin Superromance® novels and my free surprise gift. After receiving them, if I don't wish to receive anymore, I can return the shipping statement marked cancel. If I don't cancel, I will receive 6 brand-new novels every month, before they're available in stores. In the U.S.A., bill me at the bargain price of $4.69 plus 25¢ shipping and handling per book and applicable sales tax, if any*. In Canada, bill me at the bargain price of $5.24 plus 25¢ shipping and handling per book and applicable taxes**. That's the complete price, and a savings of at least 10% off the cover prices—what a great deal! I understand that accepting the 2 free books and gift places me under no obligation ever to buy any books. I can always return a shipment and cancel at any time. Even if I never buy another book from Harlequin, the 2 free books and gift are mine to keep forever.

135 HDN DZ7W
336 HDN DZ7X

Name	(PLEASE PRINT)	
Address	Apt.#	
City	State/Prov.	Zip/Postal Code

Not valid to current Harlequin Superromance® subscribers.

Want to try two free books from another series?
Call 1-800-873-8635 or visit www.morefreebooks.com.

* Terms and prices subject to change without notice. Sales tax applicable in N.Y.
** Canadian residents will be charged applicable provincial taxes and GST.
  All orders subject to approval. Offer limited to one per household.
  ® are registered trademarks owned and used by the trademark owner and or its licensee.

SUP04R   ©2004 Harlequin Enterprises Limited

You always want what you don't have

Dinah and Dottie are two sisters who grew up in an imperfect world. Once old enough to make decisions for themselves, they went their separate ways—permanently. Until now. Will their reunion seventeen years later during a series of crises finally help them create a perfect life?

My Perfectly Imperfect Life

Jennifer Archer

Available March 2006
TheNextNovel.com

HN34

Detective Maggie Skerritt is on the case again!

Maggie Skerritt is investigating a string
of murders while trying to establish her
new business with fiancé Bill Malcolm.
Can she manage to solve the case
while moving on with her life?

Spring*Break*

by *USA TODAY* bestselling author

CHARLOTTE DOUGLAS

HARLEQUIN®

Super Romance

OPEN SECRET
by Janice Kay Johnson
HSR #1332

Three siblings, separated after their parents'
death, grow up in very different homes,
lacking the sense of belonging that family
brings. The oldest, Suzanne, makes up her
mind to search for her brother and sister,
never guessing how dramatically her
decision will change their lives.

Also available:
LOST CAUSE (June 2006)

On sale March 2006
Available wherever Harlequin books are sold!

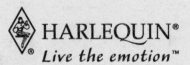

HARLEQUIN®
Live the emotion™